MERGERS & MATRIMONY

ALLISON LEIGH

W9-CBW-220

SPECIAL EDITION

Published by Silhouette Books

America's Publisher of Contemporary Romance

Acknowledgment

Special thanks and acknowledgment are given
to Allison Leigh for her contribution
to the FAMILY BUSINESS miniseries.

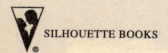

SILHOUETTE BOOKS

ISBN 0-373-24761-3

MERGERS & MATRIMONY

Copyright © 2006 by Harlequin Books S.A.

This edition published by arrangement with Harlequin Books S.A.

® and TM are trademarks of Harlequin Books S.A., used under license. Trademarks indicated with ® are registered in the United States Patent and Trademark Office, the Canadian Trade Marks Office and in other countries.

Visit Silhouette Books at www.eHarlequin.com

Printed in U.S.A.

Books by Allison Leigh

Silhouette Special Edition

*Stay... #1170
*The Rancher and the
   Redhead #1212
*A Wedding for Maggie #1241
*A Child for Christmas #1290
Millionaire's Instant Baby #1312
*Married to a Stranger #1336
Mother in a Moment #1367
Her Unforgettable Fiancé #1381
The Princess and the Duke #1465
Montana Lawman #1497
Hard Choices #1561
Secretly Married #1591

Home on the Ranch #1633
The Truth about the Tycoon #1651
All He Ever Wanted #1664
The Tycoon's Marriage Bid #1707
A Montana Homecoming #1718
Mergers & Matrimony #1761

*Men of the Double-C Ranch

ALLISON LEIGH

started early by writing a Halloween play that her grade-school class performed. Since then, though her tastes have changed, her love for reading has not. And her writing appetite simply grows more voracious by the day.

She has been a finalist in the RITA® Award and the Holt Medallion contests. But the true highlights of her day as a writer are when she receives word from a reader that they laughed, cried or lost a night of sleep while reading one of her books.

Born in Southern California, Allison has lived in several different cities in four different states. She has been, at one time or another, a cosmetologist, a computer programmer and a secretary. She has recently begun writing full-time after spending nearly a decade as an administrative assistant for a busy neighborhood church, and currently makes her home in Arizona with her family. She loves to hear from her readers, who can write to her at P.O. Box 40772, Mesa, AZ 85274-0772.

GLOSSARY

Japanese	English
hai	yes
sumimasen	I'm sorry; pardon me
Nesutotaka	Mori's (fictional) birthplace
dōmo arigatō gozaimasu	thank you very much
dōzo yoroshiku	pleased to meet you
kombanwa	good evening
kampai	cheers
sayonara	goodbye
konnichiwa	good afternoon
genkan	entry of Japanese house
ojiisan	grandfather
ohashi	chopsticks
gaijin	foreign person
Takayama	A (real) city in Japan
Sensei	teacher
Ojama shimashita	I have disturbed you—said when leaving someone's home or office
Morito (Mori) Taka	hero's name
Shiguro Taka	Mori's brother
Yukio Taka	Mori's father
Kimiko	Mori's daughter
Misaki	Mori's cousin
Sumiko	Mori's deceased wife
Akira	Mori's driver

Chapter One

She was never going to be happy again.

Why couldn't she stop that thought from circling her head?

Helen Hanson quietly rose from her chair and made her way from the wedding reception. Not a single person sitting at the crystal-bedecked table gave her a second glance. Why would they? They were all virtual strangers, connected strictly because of their connection to the bride, who'd already departed the reception with her devoted groom.

The ballroom was *filled* with people who were virtual strangers. And the ones who weren't strangers—most of them, anyway—would probably be glad of Helen's absence, should they happen to notice.

Her knees felt weak. Her heart was thudding. She very much feared she was beginning to sweat.

Perhaps she was having a hot flash.

She was only forty-one, but that didn't mean much. Menopause? Perimenopause? Simple insanity?

She pasted a pleasant smile on her face as she nodded blankly at the gazes she happened to intercept while she wound through the tables.

She might be falling apart, but she'd be damned if she'd let it show.

She was never going to be happy again.

"Stop it," she whispered to herself as she slipped out into the solitude of the corridor. The narrow heels of her Manolos sank into the thick ivory carpet and she pressed her palm flat against the silky-sheened wallpaper, steadying herself.

A young couple, laughing, rounded the corner at the end of the hall and Helen lowered her hand, managing another smile.

"Mrs. Hanson," the young woman, Samara, greeted her. "Didn't Jenny look beautiful?"

Helen nodded. Samara had been Jenny's maid of honor. "She did. As do you."

The girl flushed prettily and waved a little as her date dragged her back to the reception.

Alone again, Helen's smile faded and she walked down the hall. She wanted nothing more than to escape. To close herself in her hotel room where she could replace her couture gown with her soft fleecy sweats that were about a hundred years old and bury her head in her pillows. There, she wouldn't have to maintain the smile, the pleasant facade, the veneer of confidence that was meant to assure everyone that she knew what she was doing.

Damn you, George.

Wasn't anger one of the typical stages of grief? If it was, she didn't feel as if she'd ever get off that particular tread-board.

Her eyes burned and she started to duck into the ladies' restroom, but the sound of feminine laughter coming from inside stopped her, and she kept walking down the hall, turning corners, this way and that, only reversing her direction once again when she'd reached the kitchen and realized she was getting in the way of the busy catering staff.

She hauled in a shaking breath, smoothing her hands over the sides of her drawn-back hair.

Get a grip, Helen.

This is a happy day.

Jenny's wedding day. Your *daughter's* wedding day. To a man, a truly good man whom Helen considered a friend, even.

She closed her eyes for a moment.

It *was* a blessing. Jenny and Richard were married. And Jenny had *wanted* Helen to be there. The baby girl that she'd given up so very long ago had welcomed her.

Helen had no reason for tears.

They burned behind her eyes, anyway.

"Mrs. Hanson."

The voice was deep. Only slightly accented. It could have belonged to any man, anywhere.

She still recognized it, and it made her spine go ramrod straight.

She wasn't just anywhere. She was in Tokyo.

And he wasn't just any man.

She blinked hurriedly, then angled her chin toward him, sending him a pleasant smile. "Mr. Taka," she greeted. "I hope you and your guest are enjoying the festivity."

Morito Taka—she knew some called him Mori, but those who did were close to him, which she was not— did not have an expression of happiness on his stern countenance. He looked the way he'd looked in every business meeting he'd grudgingly taken with her. Disinterested, aloof and completely dispassionate.

"Jenny and Richard, all of us, are honored by your presence this evening." The words were as sincere as she could make them. Not only was Jenny employed by a TAKA-owned newspaper, but it had been Helen's idea for Hanson Media Group to climb into bed with TAKA. It was the only way to save the company her husband had left in shambles. But that didn't mean she had enjoyed a moment of the experience.

"You seem…disturbed." He made the comment almost unwillingly. His gaze—so dark a brown it was almost obsidian—was unwavering.

She'd seen an occasional picture of the Japanese mogul before they'd met face-to-face—all part of her research—but it had in no way armed her for just how disconcerting that gaze was, even now after months of warily circling a business deal she'd managed to engineer. A deal that would either justify George's only real desire of her, or put her family's business entirely within this man's power.

The man himself was disconcerting, when it came down to it. And she couldn't exactly pin down the reason why. Morito Taka didn't stand as tall as George—he certainly didn't top six feet the way her late husband had. At forty-seven, he was also a couple of decades younger than George had been. His dark hair was very closely cropped, as were his mustache and goatee, the latter of which sported the slightest hint of gray.

She supposed some might consider the man handsome.

She, however, was more concerned with the intentions behind those hawkish eyes.

"Women cry at weddings," she demurred. "I'm sure that isn't a habit owned wholly by Americans."

He almost smiled. She hoped. She couldn't quite tell. Not with the way the man's features were so strongly carved. There was nothing particularly friendly about Morito Taka's looks. He didn't possess the nearly constant smile of hospitality and hopefulness to please that his associates did.

Probably why she'd dreamed about him the other night. The man was a warrior. And she'd been the enemy who'd been more of a not-entirely-unwilling quarry.

Today, he wore a beautifully tailored tuxedo, in honor of the occasion. In her dream, he'd worn—

She brushed away the unwelcome thought, the way she had been for weeks. The man was only showing up in her dreams because of the power he held. It meant *nothing* more than that.

"You are not sitting with your family," he observed smoothly.

She didn't allow her smile to waver. Her three stepsons and their significants were scattered about the table seating in the reception. It might be a social event, but none of them could afford a missed opportunity for networking with the TAKA powers-that-be. But as the reception had worn on, as the champagne had flowed ever more freely, it had been natural for the family members to begin congregating.

She was always pleased to see the family together. She liked to think that during the long months since their father died, George's boys had become closer as a result of having to work together to save their heritage—Hanson Media Group. They'd all, each of them, even found happiness and love.

She also liked to think that she might have played some part in that.

But she wasn't naive, either. The boys—none of them truly boys, but that was how George had thought of them—tolerated her presence because they had to. Not because they particularly wanted to.

Jenny and Richard's reception was no exception.

"I was sitting with friends of Jenny's family."

"But not your sons."

Thank you for pointing that out. She somehow managed not to flinch. "My husband's sons," she clarified, even though he knew that fact perfectly well. He knew most every personal detail about her, including the fact that she'd had a child—Jenny—when she was little more than a child herself. When the scandal of that secret broke, he'd tried putting the kibosh on the TAKA-Hanson merger.

First of all, Jenny was an employee of TAKA. But once it had been established that she was *not* a plant of Hanson Media's, there'd still been the scandal of it.

And heaven forbid scandal touch the pristine TAKA juggernaut. Nevertheless, good business sense had obviously overridden Morito's distaste for dirty laundry, because the TAKA lawyers were still meeting with them.

"Your husband's sons," he allowed. "It must be difficult."

She waited a moment, not entirely certain which "it" he was referring to. "I'm sorry, I don't know—"

"Your loss. It is recent. Clearly, it still affects you."

George had died nine months ago. Morito undoubtedly knew that, just as she knew how long ago he'd taken charge of TAKA from his father, Yukio—a transition that hadn't gone entirely smoothly, though she'd had to dig a little to learn that fact. "Yes, it does affect me," she agreed quietly. "You lost your wife, too."

"Many years ago."

"I'm sorry."

He inclined his head a few bare inches, but it was enough to acknowledge the sentiment. She was vaguely surprised. He didn't usually seem even that human. "Your guest will be missing you," she said, hoping that he would go, and go quickly, back to the side of the very beautiful young woman who had accompanied him to the reception.

"You left because you were unwell?"

"No. I'm not unwell. I'm fine."

"One rarely seeks privacy for…happy crying. You seemed distressed."

The fact that it was this man, of all men, to notice that particular detail didn't thrill her.

The fact that her eyes started burning all over again delighted her even less. She swallowed and was very much afraid that her smile was unraveling around the edges.

His eyes narrowed and he made a soft sound under his breath. "Come." He extended one hand, long-fingered, slightly bony and definitely masculine below the perfectly short cuff. "I know a quiet place."

Now that she wasn't blocking the kitchen entrance, the corridor *was* fairly quiet. She didn't want his sympathy, or his comfort. She wanted the miracle the merger with TAKA would provide. Only then would she ever feel some semblance of contentment again.

Only then would she have proven she had at least *some* value.

His fingers touched her elbow.

Human contact. From him again, of all people.

Her eyes burned hotter. She ignored it. She should be used to ignoring her own pain; she'd been doing it for weeks. Months. Years.

She glanced up at him, the "thank you" on her lips disappearing as silently as a popping soap bubble.

His eyelashes were thick, she noted inconsequentially.

"Thank you," the tardy words emerged, soft and husky.

He bowed briefly, impersonally.

But his gaze dropped briefly, tellingly, to her lips.

She managed to keep herself from stumbling over her own high heels as he guided her along the corridor. Maybe she *was* losing her mind. She was accustomed to the way men often looked at her.

She'd never expected such a look coming from Morito Taka.

Definitely losing her mind.

Music drifted after them. They could have been in any luxurious hotel in any part of the world. But they were in an Anderson hotel, owned by the man who'd adopted her baby girl a lifetime ago.

They entered a silent elevator, yet he didn't release

her elbow. She was privately shocked, both by that fact, and by the fact that she was grateful for the support.

Even if it did come from him.

She didn't ask where they were going, or why he wasn't returning to the woman who'd accompanied him.

Instead, she stared blindly at the gleaming number display as they ascended. Her stomach felt weightless.

The elevator's doing.

Only the sensation didn't abate when the elevator stopped, and they stepped out, directly into some sort of atrium.

Plants grew in lush abandon, so different in tone from the gardens she'd become accustomed to on her visits to Tokyo. Those gardens were undeniably beautiful in their scrupulous detail and precision. This indoor garden was beautiful, but wildly so.

"Please sit." Morito directed her to an iron bench, padded in scarlet silk, placed beneath the draping fronds of some weeping tree she couldn't hope to identify.

She sat and his hand finally fell away from her elbow. He, however, didn't sit. He moved away several feet, and focused his intense attention on another tree that stood at least fifteen feet tall.

She looked upward. The ceiling was there, eventually. Most of it was glass. Her gaze moved back to Morito. His long fingers were touching a tree leaf.

Caressing it.

She looked away. Focused beyond the clusters of bushes to realize the atrium wasn't only an atrium. A hotel suite lay beyond.

"Is this your room?" She hoped the muted light masked her flush from the abrupt question.

"Hai." He gave her an inscrutable sidelong glance.

It wasn't merely a room. Nor a luxurious suite. It was a penthouse the likes of which even she was unaccustomed. And she'd grown accustomed to plenty as the wife of George Hanson.

The trophy of George Hanson.

The words circled inside her mind, mocking her.

She rose. "May I look around?" She nodded toward the living area beyond the small jungle. A winding stream of water flowed cleverly beneath the floor, enhancing the room's delineation.

"Hai."

She crossed the floor that was really a bridge over the water, and eyed the wall display opposite her.

Swords. Masks. Vases. Artifacts that looked as if they belonged in a museum somewhere rather than a hotel. She walked closer to the swords. They weren't encased under protective glass. She had the sense that she could have reached up and removed one from the wall, if she'd wanted. She stepped closer, studying the detail on the handle.

"It was my great-great-grandfather's. One of the last of the samurai."

Not just a hotel penthouse, then, but Morito's penthouse? The irony that Jenny's family owned the hotel where Mori Taka evidently *lived* struck her.

She wasn't going to wonder where his lovely companion, presumably still waiting downstairs for him, figured into the equation. "It's remarkable. The entire collection is remarkable. Also family heirlooms?"

"Yes."

"The only thing my family has of my great-grandparents' is the family bible." A bible that would have contained Jenny's name, if Helen had been stronger in the face of her father's anger. "All the births are recorded in the front of it," she elaborated.

He slid the sword off the wall. "Tradition," he murmured, studying the weapon. "It is important. Many families are forgetting that."

He held the sword comfortably. Confidently. The deadly blade was nowhere near her, yet she still felt a nervous jolt inside her. The way of the samurai had passed…hadn't it?

"And do you conquer your adversaries with the sword, still?" She kept her voice light.

His gaze transferred from the sword to her face. "Then the attorneys, yours and mine, would be left with no enjoyment at all."

It took her a moment to realize he'd made a joke. The corners of his lips were curved ever so slightly upward.

She smiled. "Very true."

Silence settled, and she realized she was still looking at the smile that so subtly touched his lips. Well-defined lips in a well-defined face.

He'd wielded a sword in her dream, too.

"Well," she said suddenly, "I should get back downstairs before they begin wondering where I've gone."

"Hai."

She was grateful he didn't voice the suspicion that nobody was likely to miss her presence no matter *how* long she was gone. "Thank you for your time, Mr. Taka. It was very kind of you."

"I am rarely kind, Mrs. Hanson." He replaced the sword on the wall. "I am certain you know that. Perhaps

I, too, needed a reason to excuse myself from the cele-bration."

"I can't imagine a man like you wanting to excuse yourself from someone as lovely as your companion." A companion who was undoubtedly twenty years—or more—his junior.

Which was the same thought most people had had upon seeing her with George.

"She is lovely," he agreed noncommittally. He walked with her across the bridge and pressed the button for the elevator. The doors immediately opened. "Your sons should be ashamed of themselves."

Whatever relaxation she might have obtained in this odd garden-penthouse-museum immediately fled. She could feel the vertebrae down her spine slipping into stiff alignment. "I don't believe my stepsons have done anything of which they should be ashamed."

She only wished they knew—could accept—just how proud she was of them. They'd all come a long way since George's death, but to say they had a warm, familial relationship was grossly overstating reality.

Helen was determined to face reality. She'd spent enough of the last several years living in something that had been anything but.

"They have a duty to you, yet they have openly shown disrespect," Morito stated.

"They are grown men who are free to express their opinions." Her tone went a little thin. Jack, the eldest, was only six years her junior. "Perhaps what you've in-terpreted as disrespect is merely open communication among the Hanson Media Group family. It was some-thing my late husband valued," she added, mentally crossing her fingers. While alive, George had never valued anyone's opinion except his own. She may have realized it during his lifetime, but it wasn't until after his death that she'd had to truly face the consequences of it. "You're a businessman, Mr. Taka. I'm sure you understand the value of many ideas being brought to the table, even when those ideas are dissenting."

"A wedding is not a meeting being held around the thirtieth-floor conference room table," he countered. "Perhaps if your husband were still alive, he would—"

"But he's not alive," she responded evenly. "I understand you would have preferred to deal with my husband, Mr. Taka." Ironic, since George had been keeping a separate set of books on Hanson Media Group, disguising the fact that the company was on the verge of ruin. "Or that you would prefer to deal with my stepson, Jack." She stepped into the elevator and turned to face him. "However, I hold the controlling interest in Hanson Media Group, so—as we say in my country—I'm afraid you're stuck with me."

His hand lifted, holding the doors from closing. "Ah, Mrs. Hanson. Do not forget." His lips curved upward again, but the motion only heightened the hardness of his high, squarely sculpted cheekbones. "Currently, you are not in your country. You are in mine."

He moved his hand and took one step back.

Helen stared at the dull reflection of herself in the doors as they closed. Her breath slowly leaked out.

"Oh, George," she whispered. "I gave you my heart and you gave me…this."

A floundering family who'd never wanted her, a sinking company and the responsibility for saving both.

Maybe she never *would* feel real happiness again. Not the kind that Jenny and Richard were experiencing. Maybe she'd never felt that in the first place, and the delirious emotions she'd felt when she'd first married George had been nothing more than a figment of her imagination.

But she'd just been firmly reminded that she didn't have the luxury of worrying about it. Not when so much stood at stake and the man who could make or break them was a modern-day warrior named Morito Taka.

Chapter Two

Trophy Wife to Media Madame?

Helen sighed, reading the headline plastered across the front of the oversize magazine.

Would the gossip never end?

The headline was accompanied by a splashy photograph of her and George from years earlier. She looked exactly what the headline proclaimed—the epitome of trophy wifedom. Not a blond hair out of place from the big, wavy affair that stretched down her back. Diamonds glittering from every point—ears, throat, wrists, fingers. The black dress was hardly sedate, either. It was cut down to there, and cut up to there. And the man beside her, George, had looked like a beefy gray bear with his proprietary arm heavy on her shoulder.

She eyed his image. She'd changed since that photo

had been taken, admittedly, mostly during the past year. No longer did she favor the big hair that George had claimed to adore. The jewelry he'd bestowed upon her, except a few narrow bracelets, her favorite watch and a tasteful necklace or two, had all been relegated to the safe back home and she didn't care if she ever wore the rest again. There were days lately when she felt as if she ought to have locked away her wedding ring, as well.

George had placed the ring on her finger all those years ago in a ceremony on an exotic beach that neither his family nor hers had even known about until after the fact.

She needed to take off the ring, yet wearing it was a reminder of what she was doing—and why.

She brushed her finger over the printed photograph. Yes, she'd changed mightily. But George hadn't.

She waited for the familiar wave of grief, but it didn't come.

She sighed again and turned the cover to the article inside, but her mind wasn't really on the rehashed story of the problems Hanson Media Group had found itself embroiled in.

Hanson Media Group had proved themselves innocent in the recent porn scandal involving their Web site, so why couldn't the gossip rags catch up with that?

She slapped the magazine closed and shoved it aside. The plate of fresh fruit and yogurt she'd ordered for breakfast held little appeal and she pushed that aside, as well, picking up her cup of coffee instead.

She probably should have stayed at her own hotel. Had her breakfast in her suite.

But she'd felt restless, particularly since Evan, Meredith, Andrew and Delia had departed for Chicago earlier that morning. Jack and Samantha had accompanied them all to the airport.

And somehow, Helen had ended up back at the Anderson hotel.

All around her, morning diners were rushing in and out of the dining room. Businessmen hunched over laptop computers while they sucked down coffee and talked on cell phones. Families waved travel brochures about and argued which sights they wanted to see that day. It was no different than any other morning she'd spent in Tokyo, yet that morning *was* different.

Jenny and Richard were married and had headed off for a brief honeymoon—all that they would allow themselves at this critical juncture of the TAKA deal—despite Helen's assurance that they should take however much time they desired.

And Helen had ended the prior evening by not endearing herself any to the exalted Morito Taka.

She rubbed her fingertip over the pain that throbbed beneath her right eyebrow. There was yet another meeting scheduled for the following afternoon with Morito and his merger and acquisitions people.

She wished it were scheduled sooner. Having to wait around more than twenty-four hours for Morito Taka to pull the plug because of her behavior the night before was wearing on her. She'd hardly slept at all and she was definitely feeling it. She wanted to snap at every person who came within five feet of her, and it was such an unaccustomed crankiness that she annoyed even herself.

She propped her elbow on the horrid gossip magazine and sipped her coffee. At the table beside her, two teenagers were trying to convince their parents that an amusement park was more appealing than the Imperial Palace garden.

Pick the garden, Helen silently commented. Amusement parks—fun though they were—abounded elsewhere, after all.

"Doing your morning reading, Mrs. Hanson?"

She jerked, spilling a drizzle of coffee over the white linen table cloth. Swallowing a curse that would surely have convinced him that she was just as coarse as he seemed to believe, she looked up at the man standing over her.

He was uncommonly tall for a Japanese man, she thought, not for the first time, and resisted the urge to stand. She might feel on more equal footing if she had, but asserting herself at the moment was probably not wise.

"Good morning, Mr. Taka." Helen summoned a pleasant smile from somewhere inside her and pinned it on her face, taking in both him and his companion— the young woman from the reception. The girl looked even more perfectly beautiful and perfectly young in the unforgiving morning light that streamed through the tall windows than she had the evening before. "Can I offer you both some coffee?" She settled her hand atop the fine silver coffeepot that sat in the middle of her table.

"I never acquired the taste for coffee," Morito said. His gaze was still on the gossip rag. His expression showed little, but Helen nevertheless sensed his disapproval.

It was the same sense she'd gotten from him since their first meeting.

The woman with him settled her long, slender hand on his arm, speaking softly. Helen's Japanese was still too shaky to follow what she said, and she made no attempt to try. Instead, she pretended not to notice the short response Morito gave to his companion, or the unmistakable credit card he removed from his pocket and handed to her. The woman bowed, expressed a musical "goodbye" to Helen, and then glided out of the dining room, her sheaf of gleaming brown hair swaying around her slender waist.

Helen looked back at Morito. "I'm sure it would take only a moment for tea to be brought, if you'd like."

"Thank you, Mrs. Hanson, but I will decline. I have business to attend to." His voice was polite, but cold. "Please enjoy your morning and your...reading."

Her molars clenched a little. "I wasn't actually enjoying this reading," she said just as politely. "But an older man in the company of a younger woman always seems to strike a popular note." Her gaze transferred briefly to his departing companion. "I'm sure you've experienced that yourself." She couldn't believe the words came out of her mouth.

His expression didn't change, but she knew with uncanny certainty that the unsubtle jab had hit its mark.

She felt no pleasure in it, however. Only more annoyance with herself for letting the man needle her. She—Hanson Media Group—*needed* this man. Why was she having such difficulty lately remembering that?

"I would feel no shame being photographed with my cousin." His voice was smooth. "As you have said, she is a lovely young woman. Now, if you will excuse me." He inclined his head and moved away before she could summon an apology.

She didn't bother cursing, now. She simply pulled out

enough yen from her minuscule purse to cover the check that had not yet been delivered, and strode after him.

Her heels clicked on the gleaming floor, joining the morning cacophony. She quickened her step, following right after him as he left the building. She was probably breaching the rules of etiquette in a dozen ways, but she couldn't let herself worry about it as she practically sprinted after him. If she didn't catch him before he entered his waiting vehicle, she wouldn't have a chance at this until their meeting the next day.

She already felt on the defensive during their meetings—she didn't need to add to it.

"Mr. Taka." She reached out and touched his arm from behind.

He stopped on the sidewalk, five yards from the teeming road, and gave her fingers a seemingly deadly look.

She let go, knowing she'd made yet another gaffe. "*Sumimasen.* I'm sorry. I made an unforgivably rude comment, Mr. Taka, and I apologize. I hope you'll accept it."

Mori stared at the blond woman standing close beside him. She seemed ignorant of the throng of people flowing around them like water separated by an annoying boulder. "Why?"

Her eyebrows drew together. She had a very narrow face, he thought. Everything about her seemed narrow. Tall. White.

She often dressed in white.

He wished he were not as aware of her as he was. He wished she were not insistent on attending every meeting concerning the takeover. She could have delegated the responsibility to someone else as she had done earlier in the process.

"Why should you accept my apology?" Her voice was low. Smooth. It possessed none of the lilting notes of the voices of the women in his life. And her gaze met his straight on. Another uncommon trait. Not just among women, but among men.

He should have found her bold gaze rude.

Instead, he found himself comparing the color of her eyes to the jade paperweight that his daughter had given him for his last birthday.

He did not like women such as Helen Hanson. But the female standing before him intrigued him, nevertheless.

His driver was waiting nearby on the sidewalk, prepared to open the door for Mori the moment he stepped toward the car. Mori ignored him. "Why does it matter to you? Our negotiations are beyond the point of worrying over small offenses." This was not strictly true. He held the power to pull out TAKA at any point he chose.

Despite his father's dissenting opinion, Mori did not yet choose to take that action.

"Then I hope you'll accept my apology because I'm not ordinarily rude." Her gaze didn't waver. "To anyone."

"So you chose to practice on me?"

A tide of pink flowed over her cheekbones. "I was irritated. Because of the magazine I was reading. I shouldn't have taken it out on you."

He understood what she was saying, but remained silent, still studying her. She wore trousers like a man, and a jacket like a man. But the white silk was closely tailored, following her lithe figure as finely as his custom-made suits fit him, and what it covered was *not* a man.

From his vantage point, he could see the pearl suspended by a thin gold chain where it rested a bare inch above the buttoned lapel of her jacket, and practically sense the velvety moistness of her skin in the morning humidity.

She took his silence for misunderstanding, though. "What I mean is that I shouldn't have turned my irritation with that ridiculous article toward you."

"The article was untrue?"

Her lips pressed together for a moment. "It was gossip."

"Fabricated?"

"Trivial, outdated and slanted. I'd hoped that publications like that would have moved on to some other topic by now rather than continuing to dwell on the past travails of Hanson Media Group."

"*Are* they in the past?" An Internet porn scandal. The revelation of a secret baby. Neither were things which he wanted even distantly associated with TAKA. No matter how advantageous it would be for TAKA to acquire Hanson's not inconsiderable U.S. assets.

She angled her head. She had high heels on her narrow feet and was only slightly shorter than he as a result. "I'm confident that they are well past, as you must be, Mr. Taka, or I doubt you and I would be having this conversation at all."

"We are having this conversation because you wanted to assure yourself of not causing me offense," he reminded.

"An assurance I still don't have," she observed. But there was no heat in the words. And her gaze still didn't swerve from his.

He found himself smiling a little. He was Japanese to his soul, but he'd had a European education. Something about the woman reminded him of those days when he had been...freer. "You are considered bold in America?"

Now, she looked wry. "I'm quite average, I'm afraid."

"That I do find difficult to believe," he admitted. If she really were an average American businesswoman, her narrow feet would not have made it past TAKA's lobby. "I accept your apology. And now you must accept mine for excusing myself." He actually felt reluctant to do so.

"Of course." She stepped back, reminding him of a tall white candle the way she stood among the navy uniforms of the cluster of schoolchildren marching by. "Until tomorrow afternoon, then." One of the children nearly bumped into her, and a quick smile lit her features as they avoided collision.

The vestiges of the smile crinkled her nose and revealed a faint dimple in her cheek as she looked from the child back to him.

The smile was quite unlike the smoothly practiced ones she usually exhibited.

Instead of moving to his car, he stood there. He had seen the untouched plate of food on her table when he and Misaki had stopped. The *single* plate of food.

When they were sitting in a conference room, Helen Hanson was a woman surrounded by family and business associates. But to share her morning coffee and fruit, she'd had no one.

Again.

"You did not finish your meal."

Now, her bold gaze dropped. He knew, in her case, it was not a sign of respect, but an indicator of avoidance.

"I'd had enough," she said. "Thank you, Mr. Taka, for your time. I look forward to meeting with you again." She placed her hands on her legs and bowed.

He had things to do. Responsibilities. There was no reason to prolong their impromptu meeting.

"As do I," he replied automatically. "Do you have plans for today?" Whatever they would be, they would not involve any member of TAKA. They did not have another meeting scheduled until the following day. Mori expected to spend at least a portion of his afternoon allaying his father's latest battery of concerns where the takeover was concerned.

Helen had straightened and once again, her expression showed some slight bewilderment. Not surprising. He was not given to pointless conversations. It was not his way to be rude, of course, but neither was it his way to waste time. He had no time to waste, generally.

"I thought I might do some sightseeing," she said. "I read about a festival being held this week. I—I'm afraid I can't recall the name of the location. I have it written down back at my hotel."

"Rarely a week passes when there is not some kind of festival."

"It has something to do with the leaves beginning to change."

"Ah." He nodded. "Your sons will accompany you?"

The bewilderment cooled, and he found himself regretting his voiced assumption when her smile went from spontaneous to practiced.

"My stepsons have their own plans," she said, backing away yet another step. "As well they should. I've delayed you long enough, Mr. Taka. Again, my apologies."

His life had been an endless series of social courtesies where apologies were rote. For an American woman like Helen Hanson, he doubted that was the case. "I have some free time this morning. Perhaps you would allow me to be your guide?"

Her lips parted in surprise, but he gave her credit for recovering quickly enough. "I would be honored, Mr. Taka."

He was fairly confident that honor had little to do with her acquiescence. She wanted his cooperation in the TAKA boardroom.

"Very good," he said. "My driver and I will take you to your hotel to retrieve your necessities."

"Thank you, but that won't be necessary." She held up a tiny clutch, not much bigger than a wallet. "I have everything I need in here. My room key and passport and such. Not that it's a key, of course. Just one of those credit-card type things. I'm forever having to get a new one at my hotel. I seem to demagnetize them or something." The rush of words halted abruptly. Pink color rode her cheekbones again and she stepped toward the car.

His driver immediately opened the rear door and Mori watched Helen slide into the limousine. She sat down first and then drew in her legs.

Her pant legs rode up a few inches as she did so, treating him to a brief glimpse of very slender, very delicate ankles.

He stared over the hood of the vehicle, not seeing any of the traffic quietly congesting the street or the pedestrians streaming along the sidewalks.

Evidently, he had gone insane, just as his father kept accusing.

He restrained the urge to loosen his tie and haul in a

deep breath as he moved to the car and climbed in beside Helen.

She sent him a smile that looked as uneasy as he felt.

Then Akira closed the door softly, and there was only Mori and Helen, seemingly shut off from the rest of the world.

He flicked open the buttons holding his jacket closed and stared straight ahead.

The smell of her—something sophisticated but oddly light—filled his head.

He had been accomplished in the art of small talk since he had worn short pants. But summoning inane banter just then seemed to require tremendous effort. "Have you done much sightseeing?" He managed to glance her way, politely enquiring.

Her hands were folded neatly together in her lap. She wore an enormous diamond ring on her wedding ring finger.

"Not as much as I'd like," she admitted. "I feel as though I've spent more time on airplanes traveling back and forth from Chicago to Tokyo than actually staying put long enough here to see as much as I've wanted to."

"You…enjoy Tokyo?"

"It's a fascinating city. I'm always so surprised that it's as quiet as it is." She looked away, out the side window. Her hair was pulled back in a ponytail that revealed the nape of her neck.

"Quiet?" He faced ahead again and when she turned forward once more, his gaze seemed to meet hers in the subtle reflection provided by the smoked partition separating them from the driver.

"For such a large city, I find it remarkably quiet.

There is traffic noise, certainly, but rarely have I heard a horn honk. It's nothing like Chicago."

"No, it is not."

"You've been to Chicago?"

"Occasionally. It, too, is an interesting city."

She smiled faintly. Even in the dim partition, the reflection of it was bright. "Are you being polite?"

"Yes."

"What did you *really* think about Chicago?"

"Noisy. Intrusive." He switched his gaze from the reflection to the real thing. "Impolite."

Her eyes glinted with humor, which surprised him.

Ordinarily, she was very circumspect, highly intelligent and mostly aloof.

Until he had found her hiding tears, that was.

Then, she had seemed wholly human.

"I find it vibrant and endlessly entertaining," she argued pleasantly.

"Also true."

Her eyebrows rose. "Really?"

"I enjoy Chicago when I visit."

"How often do you get to the U.S.?"

"A few times a year. I am in London more often."

"On business or pleasure?"

"Ah. To me, Mrs. Hanson, business *is* pleasure."

Her sudden frown was quickly smoothed away. "That's something my husband used to say."

"You miss him a great deal?"

Her lashes swept down for a moment, hiding those jade eyes. "Of course." Then she turned and looked out the window again. "I love Chicago, too. But I must say I'm becoming quite fond of Tokyo."

"Have you always lived in Chicago?"

"Oh, no." The moment of awkwardness seemed to ease. "I come from New York state, originally. I moved to Chicago when I was a young woman."

"You are still a young woman."

"Kindly put and appreciated. Particularly by a woman who's just watched her—" she faltered only slightly "—grown daughter get married."

"You will be a beautiful woman when you are eighty," he said diplomatically. Truthfully.

Her lips twitched a little as if she were trying not to laugh. "I'd accuse you of flattery, but that seems out of character."

For the first time in longer than he could remember, *he* chuckled. The sound startled her as much as it did him. "True."

After a moment that lasted longer than it should, they both looked away from each other.

The limousine pulled into the park, where a throng of people had already gathered. When Mori stepped out of the car, a breeze had sprung up, helping in a small way to alleviate the humidity. He turned back and took Helen's hand to help her from the vehicle.

She stepped out beside him, and he released her, pretending not to notice the way she rubbed her palms together, as if she, too, felt the lingering heat. Above their heads, leaves from the trees flitted in the air like gently burnished confetti.

She craned her head, avidly taking in the small, orderly garden that was lined with Japanese maples. "It is so beautiful here." The words were little more than a sigh.

"Yes."

Only Mori was not looking at the trees.

He was looking at her.

Chapter Three

They walked together.

Mostly in silence at first, which suited Helen just fine. She wasn't accustomed to feeling tongue-tied, yet being in Morito Taka's presence definitely had that effect.

"In a few weeks, the turning of the leaves will be at its peak," he told her. His hand lightly touched the small of her back as they stepped around a cluster of young women and children.

In a few weeks, she hoped the merger would be complete. "We have the fall colors at home, too. My home is surrounded by trees, in fact." An architectural magazine had once described the grounds around George Hanson's estate as the forest protecting the media king.

Only recently had Helen admitted to herself that staying alone in the house had become more than she could

bear. It had been one thing when she'd only been griev-
ing the loss of her husband.

As if such a thing could ever be an "only."

But when she'd believed she'd *only* been the woman
called late one night and told that her husband had suffered
a massive heart attack in his office, it had been simpler.

Not that George had betrayed her with another woman.

In a way, that might have been simpler, too.

No, George had betrayed her with the very company
that he'd charged her with saving. The company that had
been his *real* love.

And when she'd learned that fact, staying alone in his
mausoleum of a house had become increasingly difficult.

Being near his personal effects—she still hadn't had
the heart to clear them away—had become a mockery
instead of a comfort. The house with the soaring,
gleaming windows that afforded one a spectacular view
of their own personal "forest" had become more of a
prison than a haven.

"Mrs. Hanson?"

She dragged her thoughts together with more effort
than it usually took. Morito was clearly waiting for her
to accompany him along the walkway which forked in
front of them.

"Call me Helen," she said, not particularly caring if
she were committing yet another breach of etiquette or
not with the request. She stepped forward, catching her
heel on the edge of the pavers.

His hand steadied her. "Are you all right?"

No. She was insane. She was stressed. She was…
alone in a world crammed full of people. "Perfectly,"
she lied, her voice bright. "Is that row of lanterns

hanging from the trees decorative, or do they ever
light up?"

"They are lit every evening." His dark gaze didn't
transfer from her face to the lantern display, however.
And she felt herself flushing.

Like some foolish schoolgirl.

It was embarrassing.

"I imagine it's beautifully picturesque."

But he clearly wasn't interested in the visual appeal
of the lanterns. "Why is it that you choose to involve
yourself in your late husband's business when you could
be doing anything else that interests you?"

"Is that why you offered to play tour guide? To try
and scare me off the merger?"

"I was under the impression that nothing scared
you—" his hesitation was barely noticeable "—Helen."

Her throat constricted on a swallow. *Be careful of
what you ask for, because you might get it.*

She unbuttoned her jacket and slid out of it, folding
it over her arm. When she looked up at him, he was
looking at her silky white camisole. It was a perfectly
decent garment, with double spaghetti-straps and a
neckline high enough to afford zero cleavage.

She still felt naked under that look of his.

But donning her jacket once more was out of the
question. First, it was too warm and humid. Second, he
would then know he unsettled her.

The man had the upper hand all too often and she was
tired of it.

Would it equalize them if he knew *she'd* been at the
root of bringing the American company known as Hanson
Media Group to TAKA's attention in the first place?

Would he respect the bold action, or would he detest it *for* that very boldness?

"I have plenty of fears," she assured. "And I'm in charge at Hanson Media Group because my late husband believed that's where I should be." Only after he was gone, though. Never while he'd been alive.

"Is it where *you* want to be?"

"Is heading TAKA where *you* want to be?" she returned.

"It is my duty."

"As Hanson Media Group is mine." The conversation wasn't going anywhere she wanted it to go. "But enough of duty." She smiled brightly. "What do you do for enjoyment?"

"Walk in a garden with an interesting woman."

Her breathing hitched a little. But she was too mature to be swayed by pretty words. In the beginning, George had had plenty of lovely sentiments. Ultimately, though, they'd meant nothing. "You're too polite to describe me as what you really think."

He was definitely amused. The lines fanning out from his eyes crinkled slightly into evidence. "And that would be?"

She gave it a moment of thought. "A jarring woman."

"Jarring?"

"Like the sound of metal scraping over concrete."

"Ah." He caught a blowing leaf right out of midair. "No. I do not think so." Holding the leaf by the stem, he twirled it slowly between his fingers. "You are not the norm."

"Not in Japan."

"Not in Japan," he confirmed.

She supposed it was progress that he didn't lecture her about what was the norm in his world.

"I enjoy my own garden," he said after they'd walked a while. "My daughter. Though her insatiable curiosity and sense of mischief is a trial at times. Mountain climbing. And, surprisingly—" he gave her a sidelong look "—sparring with an interesting woman."

Then, while she was feeling rather speechless over his uncharacteristically personal comments, he handed her the leaf.

"It is time we return."

She nodded silently, and they turned back in the direction of the waiting limousine.

It seemed only minutes before she was dropped off at her own hotel. As he'd done at the park, Mori waved off the chauffeur and alighted from the vehicle first, then turned and gave his hand to her.

She steeled herself, then placed her palm against his. His long tanned fingers closed around hers, and she joined him on the sidewalk. The moment she was upright, he let go of her, which was a good thing if she wanted to be able to continue breathing in any sort of normal fashion.

She moved her jacket from one arm to the other, keeping hold of the leaf, as well, then repeated the bow that she'd spent quite some time privately perfecting. "Thank you again, Mr. Taka, for your time. I look forward to our next meeting tomorrow."

He bowed, as well, and stepped to the car, looking like some sort of lithe tiger as he sank down on the sleek leather seat. He looked at her from the darkened, air-conditioned interior. "Please call me Mori."

Then he pulled the door shut and the limousine pulled from the curb to be swallowed among the stream of nonstop traffic.

"Do you require assistance, Hanson-san?" The uniformed doorman approached her.

Helen dragged her attention from the departing vehicle and shook her head, giving the doorman a distracted smile as she headed into the hotel. "Thank you, no."

The attorneys always seemed to be the first ones to arrive. When Helen stepped into the TAKA conference room the next afternoon, there were half a dozen of them already there. Including Jack. He noticed her arrival and headed toward her, lowering his head a little when he stopped beside her. "You weren't in your room last night."

Curiosity had her lifting her eyebrows. "I went to the gym."

"Samantha tried reaching you for a few hours."

Helen hadn't received any phone messages. "Is something wrong?"

His handsome face looked slightly uncomfortable. "We thought you might join us for dinner."

Bless Samantha. Helen knew the invitation would have to have been instigated by her old friend, now married to Jack. "I'm sorry," she said sincerely. "I would have been happy to join you." Instead, she'd sweated for an hour with free weights and stretched herself into contortions with Pilates. She'd wanted to wear herself out enough to sleep well, and for the most part, she'd succeeded.

She'd slept quite well.

She'd also dreamed quite vividly. Even now, remembering, she could feel warmth beneath her skin.

"You're looking flushed." Jack's sharp gaze missed nothing. "Are you sick?"

Not so long ago, Helen would have believed that Jack would be happy if she'd said she was, for then he could insist she miss the meeting. It had been bad enough that he'd been thrust into helming Hanson Media after his father died, an act that had pulled him away from his own successful legal career. But it had been an even more bitter pill to have the stepmother he'd never had any use for become, essentially, his boss when George's will had left her with the majority interest in the company.

In the past few months, Jack had not necessarily become fond of her, but he'd at least realized she wasn't the dimwitted blond bimbo he'd once believed her to be. The merger with TAKA had been her idea, and he'd seen the value in it.

Hanson Media Group could not continue to function on its own. George's mismanagement had been too devastating. But the merger with TAKA would ensure that the family business would continue to exist. His heritage would not be lost. It would certainly be changed, but they *would* continue. Hundreds of Hanson employees would keep their jobs. George's boys would still have their inheritance, as would their children, once they began arriving. And considering that Delia, Andrew's bride, was quite pregnant, that wouldn't be far off now.

"I'm fine, Jack, just anxious to get this underway." She glanced around the room, then at her watch. "Everyone is here but Mori." The man wasn't usually late.

"Mori?" Jack repeated. "Since when is he *Mori?*"

"Ever the lawyer," Helen tsked lightly, patting his arm. No one would be seated around the table until the head honcho appeared, so she nodded toward the tea tray set up on a sleek ebony credenza. Today, the tray was manned by a thin woman who was as adept at fading into the background as the other voiceless attendants had been. "Do you want to start off with some tea?"

"I could float a steamer on all the tea I've drunk lately," Jack muttered under his breath.

Helen hid a smile. "The details shouldn't take much longer to finalize, then you can get back to normal life."

He looked disbelieving.

She didn't feel so much like smiling then. Was he so jaded that he couldn't believe that he wasn't sentenced to Hanson Media duty for the rest of his days?

She flipped open her leather notepad and drew out the gold pen that had been in her possession ever since she'd plucked it and a sealed envelope bearing her name out of George's personal effects in his desk. She jotted a note on her daily journal to try reaching Judge Henry again back in Chicago, and as she did so, Mori entered the room, three young men dogging his heels as they nodded and listened intently to whatever it was that he was saying. His Japanese was too rapid and low for Helen to follow, but the words certainly had his minions scurrying when he finished.

His gaze traveled impersonally over the occupants of the room—all of whom had seemed to stand just a little straighter when he'd appeared—as he walked straight to the head of the conference table and rested his fingertips on the highly glossed ebony surface.

If Helen had hoped for his glance to linger when it reached her, she'd have been sorely disappointed. He gave her no more regard than he did the tea attendant who silently placed a tall glass of water beside him after he'd seated himself.

She told herself she wasn't disappointed and that was that.

This *was* a business meeting, after all. Not an unexpected stroll through a park.

The rest of the attendees arranged themselves around the table, reminding Helen, not for the first time, of soldiers assuming battle positions. She was sitting to Mori's left, with Jack nearest the man. The rest of the left side was occupied by her team. The right side of the table was comprised of TAKA representatives.

She wondered what the right side would do if the left pulled out a handful of rubber bands and began shooting them across the wide, wide table.

She grabbed the gold pen and banished her silly thoughts. Each place setting around the table had been furnished with a packet of materials bound within a slick cover that featured only the TAKA logo.

After a nod from his brother Mori, Shiguro Taka, a more familiar face at these meetings than Mori, smiled across the table and reached for his packet. "Good afternoon. We will turn to your marked pages, and continue from our last meeting. Mr. Hanson—" his attention focused on Jack "—you will note that the changes you required have been incorporated in this revision. They are so noted." The explanation was redundant, since they'd all been down this road before. Helen didn't bother pointing out that the last round of revisions had been at her demand, not Jack's.

As long as the concessions had been made in favor of Hanson, she was happy. The last thing she wanted to do was lose even twelve percent of their Chicago staff because of outsourcing their accounting department to TAKA headquarters.

She followed the text of the voluminous document as Jack and Shiguro laboriously went point by point through the pages. The afternoon light was lengthening through the tall windows lining the wall when, nearly thirty pages later, she silently reached over to Jack's copy and circled an item.

Shiguro kept reading aloud as Jack glanced at her. She shook her head, mouthing "No."

He nodded and looked across the table at Shiguro. "I'm sorry, Mr. Taka. Our position with regard to the philanthropic budget remains unchanged. These funds are raised and administered by employees within the Chicago headquarters. It is an employee-driven effort that benefits the community and Hanson Media has always given a dollar-for-dollar match."

Shiguro's pleasant expression didn't change. "A four-million-dollar employee giving campaign is an admirable accomplishment, Mr. Hanson, one that requires no additional corporate contributions."

"Since its inception, Hanson Media Group has pledged equal support to that of its employees," Helen spoke before Jack could. "It is that kind of involvement in our local communities that has helped Hanson maintain its strong foothold in the marketplace. The consumer buying one of our publications believes we're in partnership with them in making a better community. It's not just good citizenship—it's good marketing."

"Expensive marketing," Shiguro countered, clearly willing to argue the point.

Helen was prepared for it, though. Goodness knows she'd argued with Jack and her own team over the matter often enough. Four million dollars a year *was* a lot of money, particularly for a company that had just narrowly avoided bankruptcy.

Mori murmured something to Shiguro, and the other man's expression tightened. But he nodded. "A fifty-percent match."

Jack started to speak. Helen touched his arm. "One hundred percent," she said.

"Mrs. Hanson." Shiguro shook his head almost pityingly as he sat back in his seat. "You must not understand the situation."

"Sixty percent," Mori said, cutting off his brother.

Helen looked Mori's way, and found his gaze focused on her. She wished she'd accepted the tea or glass of water when the girl had offered it, since her mouth felt impossibly dry. "Ninety."

She heard Jack murmur her name under his breath. "Be reasonable," he added quietly.

She remained silent.

"Mrs. Hanson," Shiguro interjected. "TAKA believes in contributing to its community as well. Our charitable giving—"

"—reached an incredibly generous three point seven percent of the proceeds for your last three fiscal years."

Shiguro clearly did not appreciate being interrupted,

least of all by her. "Sixty percent." He repeated his brother's concession.

She shook her head.

All around the table, members on both the right and left sides began shifting.

"If we agree to table this item for today," Jack suggested, "we could continue?"

Helen could have sat there all evening and argued her side, but she knew in the scheme of things, the point was a relatively minor one to most everyone but her. "We can resolve it another time," she agreed. The practice wasn't uncommon to their negotiations.

Shiguro glanced at Mori, and seemed to take his silence for assent, because he focused once more on their agreement. "We will continue, then, in the following section." Papers rustled around the table as pages were turned.

"The changeover in all branding to the TAKA brand will be accomplished within twelve months," Shiguro read, glancing at Jack over the top of the reading glasses he'd pushed onto his nose.

Helen carefully set her pen down on the center of her notepad.

Shiguro continued. "All media relations regarding the acquisition of Hanson Media Group will be directed through the Tokyo office."

At that, even Jack started shaking his head. "That is neither feasible nor practical."

"It is TAKA's belief that—"

"This is not an acquisition," Helen reminded him, for what felt like the millionth time. That was the tightrope they constantly walked—to retain as much control of Hanson Media as they possibly could while availing themselves of the power and positioning of the Japanese juggernaut. "The *branding* of Hanson Media Group carries more weight with Americans than TAKA does. By exchanging one for the other, we'll be alienating the very people who keep us in business. These are the people who purchase HMG periodicals. Listen to HMG radio stations. Subscribe to HMG online services. To them, TAKA is just another name. HMG is part of American culture."

"As TAKA is not acquiring your radio stations, we are not concerned with that," Shiguro said. "And while I'm sure your opinion is heartfelt, every acquisition of TAKA bears the TAKA name."

"Until now. And could we refrain from using the term *acquisition?* This—" she hefted the bound document up a few inches and let it drop heavily on the table "—is a merger."

Shiguro gave her a condescending look before transferring his focus to Jack, then to the raft of legal eagles to Helen's side. "This *acquisition* will be handled in the same manner as we've always—"

"Mrs. Hanson is correct." Mori's words stopped Shiguro's midstream. "A study was commissioned a few years ago on the importance of branding in the American marketplace. Perhaps Hanson Media Group is not up to the level to which some soft drinks or photocopiers have risen, but it was nevertheless one of the most widely recognized corporate names in that area of the country."

Helen slowly picked up her pen again. She had a print out of the salient points from that particular study tucked in a pocket of her notepad. Now, she wouldn't even have to pull it out.

Her gaze lingered on Mori, but she directed her comment toward the other side of the table. "Hanson Media Group may have had some faltering moments this past year—" a mild understatement "—but that does not negate the positive public image it has held for decades. TAKA will be benefiting more in the U.S. under our brand, and there is not one person around this table who does not recognize that fact." She let her gaze travel that table, resting briefly on each person in turn. "We would, however, consider changing the name to Hanson North America. With the divestiture of our radio division prior to the merger with TAKA, we could roll out the amended corporate name and play on the broadening to an international status."

Mori gave a slight nod. Nobody argued with her suggestion. Shiguro was surprisingly quiet.

"Hanson North America. I will have our PR department get in touch with yours to coordinate the details. The item regarding branding will be amended," Mori said and that was that. They moved on to the next paragraph.

Jack gave her a sideways look of approval and Helen wanted to sit on her hands to keep from shaking with triumph. Instead, she just kept a tight grip on George's gold pen.

There was no sunlight pouring through the windows by the time the meeting ended. Helen had a stiff ache in the small of her back from sitting for so long. She'd taken pages of notes, and argued several more points, not all of which she won, but overall, she was intensely satisfied with the accomplishments of the day.

And the evening.

"I suppose I'm going to have to go out and drink with

these people again," Jack murmured to her as everyone rose and began talking about anything under the sun as long as it was not mergers and acquisitions. "I'd rather get back to Samantha."

Helen didn't doubt it, but she knew there was no point in reminding Jack that if he was invited out, he couldn't possibly refuse, for to do so would be offensive.

Shiguro was making his way toward them, his customary smile back in place. He did not present the physical presence that his brother did, but he was nevertheless a striking man. "My brother wishes a moment with you, Mrs. Hanson, if you would be so kind?"

Helen ignored the surprised look she received from Jack. "Of course." She excused herself and headed toward Mori. Behind her, she heard Shiguro courteously ask Jack and the rest of the Hanson team—all men—to join him for drinks. She didn't let it bother her that she was not included in the invitation. It wasn't the first time she'd been excluded, and she had no real desire to beat the bars for several hours before engaging in an argument over who would take care of the check, which—according to Jack—was how most of those excursions ended. That particular debate was primarily an expected exercise in courtesy. TAKA always picked up the tab in the end no matter how many times Jack insisted on getting it "next time."

Mori stood near the door, in conversation with two other men. The assistant who'd accompanied him, and who'd been the minute-taker of the meeting, was standing just behind him, taking more copious notes.

Helen waited to the side, not wanting to interrupt him. She was well aware of Jack still watching her even as he conversed with Shiguro. Of course he would be curious why Mori would request to speak with her. It wasn't a common occurrence. In fact, it was a first-time occurrence.

Her eldest stepson caught her eye. More than curious, she decided, giving Jack an almost imperceptible shake of her head. Jack was definitely...disapproving.

And, sadly, that *wasn't* uncommon at all. She ought to have been used to it by now. George's boys had never accepted her marriage to their father despite her best efforts at forging some sort of relationship with them. She really ought to have developed a thicker hide by now.

"Mrs. Hanson." Mori touched her elbow and she nearly jumped right out of her skin.

She laughed a little, meeting his intensely dark gaze. Mrs. Hanson. Not Helen. So much for progress. "You caught me woolgathering, I'm afraid."

He tilted his head slightly. "Daydreaming."

"Ah...well, yes."

His lips lifted ever so faintly. "I hope they were pleasant, then. The daydreams." His gaze flicked briefly to the darkened windows before returning to her face. "Though the day is already sleeping."

She could feel Jack's gaze boring a hole in her back. "Was there something specific you wished to speak with me about?"

"Yes." He looked beyond her. "Your son must have made a formidable attorney. He looks fierce."

"Jack is well-suited to the law," she understated. Jack *had* been formidable. He still was, for that matter. No more than the man standing beside her, however.

"You are tired?"

She hesitated, thrown by the directly personal comment. "It's been a long day." Preceded by many long days. "But I'm pleased with the results."

Now, there was a definite glint in his eyes. "I'm certain that you are," he said mildly. "Shiguro is perhaps less pleased."

Helen smiled faintly, not commenting. They watched Shiguro and his group make their way out of the conference room, Jack among them.

When their voices no longer could be heard in the corridor, however, the vast quietness of the conference room pressed in on Helen.

As did the fact that she and Mori were very much alone.

"Did you wish to join them?"

Once again, she was surprised by his perception, and then annoyed with herself for *being* surprised. The man was far too observant. "No," she admitted.

"Shiguro has a liking for karaoke that not everyone shares."

The image of Jack in a karaoke bar made Helen's lips lift. But she still didn't know what had prompted Mori's request to speak with her.

"You are…feeling better?"

Caution leaked into her. "I'm quite well, thank you."

"Our negotiations have progressed more slowly than we expected."

She considered reminding him that he was the primary reason for that, with his objections that had nearly derailed the deal more than once. "Things worthwhile aren't often come by easily."

He nodded slightly. "I tell my daughter that when she does not want to study."

It was hard envisioning the severe businessman as a father, though she'd already known he was one. "How old is your daughter?"

"Twelve. For another few months, anyway."

"Ah. Almost a teenager. Are you prepared for that?" she asked lightly.

"Dreading," he deadpanned. "Will you dine with me?"

Her pen slipped from her fingers.

He stooped and retrieved it before she could, and held it up to study. "I have noticed that you are never without this. What do the initials signify?"

She took it when he handed it to her, and slid it into her portfolio. "My husband's name." She didn't really want to talk about the pen she'd given George or its significance. "Was there something particular about the merger you wanted to discuss?"

"Over dinner, you mean."

"Yes."

"Not everything concerns business."

"Right now, for me it does." The admission came without thought.

He slid the portfolio out of her surprised hands. "That is a pity."

She eyed him when he cupped her elbow and urged her toward the door. "Why?"

"You are a beautiful woman."

She didn't presume that he meant it as a compliment. "I suppose you believe I should be more concerned with nonbusiness pursuits?" They'd arrived at the elevator and he released her elbow as he pushed the call button. "Maybe you think I'm only suited for finding another husband who can keep me in diamonds and Botox."

"You prefer a marriage of emotion, I suppose."

The elevator doors slid open and she stepped inside. "Contrary to popular belief, I did marry for love. And, quite honestly, I can't imagine feeling that way again."

Mori followed her into the elevator and pressed the button. "My daughter claims she never wants to marry."

"She is only twelve."

"When I was her age, my parents had already arranged my marriage." He looked from the lights of the floor display to her. "Kimiko wants only to move to America and be famous."

"Doing what?"

He seemed to shrug without ever truly moving a muscle. "I think she has not decided on that, yet. As long as it is very…American."

Her stomach swooped a little, a result of the elevator's rapid descent. "And you disapprove."

"She would do better to apply her passionate interest to her schoolwork than to whatever fad currently has your country in its grip."

At least his voice had lightened. She smiled in response. "Now *that* sounds like a typical twelve-year-old."

He smiled a little, too, but didn't comment.

She could guess what he was thinking, though. Probably the same thing she was. That her only experience with twelve-year-old children had been when *she* was one. They both knew she'd never been involved in her own daughter's life when she was twelve.

The elevator slowed abruptly and the doors slid open to the silent, cavernous lobby. The only occupants were three security guards, who stood and greeted them as they passed and stepped out into the evening.

The same car as the other day waited curbside and Mori headed toward it. "Come. We will eat and not discuss business. That can wait for the next time we sit around the conference table."

Her stomach swooped again, but this time she couldn't blame it on the elevator. "Then what will we talk about?"

He lifted his hand toward her, palm upward. His hooded gaze settled on her face. "Something will come to us."

Involvement with this man over anything that *wasn't* business—even something as simple as a walk in the park or dinner—was a mistake.

She knew it. She *knew* it.

But she stepped forward anyway and put her hand on his.

Chapter Four

Mori was not certain what had prompted him to ask the woman to dinner. The same nonsensical thinking that had prompted him to accompany her to the park.

Both decisions were inexplicable.

Except that he could not rid himself of the image of Helen, alone once again.

She was silent as Akira drove them away from the TAKA building. Was she merely looking out the window at the passing lights, or was she wondering as much as he was *what* they were doing there together?

Business did indeed make strange bedfellows.

"I thought we would go to the Anderson hotel." He finally broke the silence. "The restaurant there is admirable." International food and international clientele. Helen would be quite at home.

"Yes, it is a lovely restaurant. I've eaten there several times."

There was nothing in her voice to indicate dissatisfaction, nothing in the composed expression revealed by the on-off flicker of neon as they drove. For some reason, he still sensed it.

"It is uncomfortable for you to go there? The Andersons are—"

"Oh, no," she cut in quickly. "I'm very comfortable at the hotel's restaurant."

Even if it was owned by the man who had adopted her daughter.

She did not voice the words, but Mori added them anyway.

She made a little sound. "With you having a suite there, I certainly don't have to tell you how wonderful the restaurant is. But it's been comfortable for me. Very…Western. I don't have to worry about showing off how inept I still am eating with *o-hashi*. It's silly, and nothing for you to concern yourself with, truly. I just…well, I find I'm missing my own kitchen."

"You cook?"

She turned a little, until she was facing him more squarely. Her hair gleamed like a beloved pearl in the dim light. "I've been known to attempt it." Her voice was slightly dry. "I wasn't always married to a man who had a raft of household staff. George never understood that I actually liked fixing meals. That was Cook's job and that was that."

"Sumiko—my wife—preferred to be the organizer."

Her smile widened. "Plan the meals, but leave the actual preparing of it to the chef?"

He did not know why he had mentioned his wife. Particularly when he so rarely thought of her. "Yes. It is refreshing to have a meal at home." His words were sincere. Though he had not been to his own home outside the city in many weeks. "I also enjoy the kitchen. When are you planning your return to the United States?"

She took the abruptness of his question in stride. "Looking forward to getting rid of me?"

"Shiguro may be feeling some anticipation."

She laughed softly, then waved her hand. "I'm sorry. I know I shouldn't laugh. Your brother is a credit to the TAKA organization."

Shiguro was. But Mori was not unaware of his brother's annoyance with having Helen involved in their negotiations or that he was an easier mark for their father when it came to influencing him against the Hanson deal.

"Actually, I was thinking how long it had been since I was at *my* home."

"Where is that?"

"A few hours north of Tokyo. A very small village where I was born."

"The original Taka-ville?"

He smiled faintly. "Something like that. Nesutotaka. My mother's home is there though my father prefers to spend most of his time at their apartment here. He finds it difficult to be too far away from the office."

"You succeeded him only a few years ago?"

He nodded. "We agreed to speak of other matters," he reminded.

"So we did. Tell me about Nesutotaka."

"You would consider it…old-fashioned. It is wooded and very green. No proper roads."

"No concrete high-rises?"

"The only high-rise is the mountain that overlooks the village."

"It sounds lovely."

"Kimiko, my daughter, loathes it."

"Kimiko." Helen sounded the name softly. "What does it mean?"

"Essentially, beautiful child."

"Kimiko," she repeated again, nodding. "What a wonderful name. I suppose for a twelve-year old girl, Nesutotaka is pretty tame."

"Dull was the word she last used, I believe. She is most happy to stay at her school, or at my father's home. He does not indulge her liking for the more modern culture, but he has television, at least."

"Does she stay with you at all here in Tokyo?"

"My duties are not very interesting to her, either," he said drily. "She stays with me very rarely."

She fell silent for a moment. "You must miss her."

"Yes."

"Well, perhaps she'll grow up and work side by side with you at TAKA. Be the first women in a senior management position there."

"She will make a suitable marriage."

Helen made a soft sound. "Have you already picked out her groom?"

"There are families I would consider." His father was already greatly displeased that the matter had not been fully arranged.

"And what about what Kimiko wants?"

"Kimiko will please her father."

Her brows rose a little. "Oddly enough, you just sounded like *my* father. He was adamant about what I would or wouldn't do, as well."

"It is a father's duty to see to the well-being of his children."

"I'd rather think of it as a father's privilege." Her voice had noticeably cooled.

"You are American. You have no reason to understand this thinking."

"I understand that my father ruled his family with an iron fist, because that was his *duty.* I don't think he once considered what was truly best for our welfare."

"Our?"

"My mother. My brother. Me."

"You are close?"

She shook her head. "My mother died several years ago. My father still lives in a small town in upstate New—" She broke off when the phone in the console discreetly beeped.

"Please excuse me." He answered, knowing he was not going to like the results as soon as he heard the voice of Kimiko's headmaster. He listened, watching Helen from the corner of his eyes.

She had looked out the window again in a polite attempt at offering him some privacy.

"I will come by tonight," he cut off the headmaster's stream of excited chatter and disconnected the call.

Yes, he missed his daughter, but he did *not* miss Kimiko's present path of mischief.

"Problem?"

"An inconvenience."

"If you need to pass on dinner, I'll understand."

Canceling at this juncture would be unacceptable. "The headmaster of my daughter's school. He will wait."

"Is she all right?"

Did he seem so cold that she thought he would ignore Kimiko if she *were not?* "Until she must face her father, she is."

"And it is none of my business. I'm sorry if it sounded as if I were prying."

Her voice had regained its formal cadence. The pearl that glowed from human contact now looked cool and distant. No less lovely, but far less valuable.

"The school is near here. If you would not mind delaying our dinner a short while, I can attend to the matter, and we can dine after."

She made no movement, yet her demeanor immediately softened again. "I don't mind in the least. But your daughter may wish to have dinner with you."

He doubted it. He pushed the intercom button that connected the rear of the limo to Akira. "Stop at Kim's school."

"Hai."

"I hope she isn't in very much trouble," Helen said after a moment. "Your expression is...fierce."

He realized he was frowning and tried to stop.

A smile played around Helen's lips as she witnessed his effort. "There is an expression. 'Turn that frown upside down.' Have you heard it?"

"No."

She made an exaggerated frown and touched her finger to the corner of her lip, nudging upward. The frown became a smile.

"Silliness." Kimiko would undoubtedly be enthralled with the woman.

"I think everyone needs a little silliness in their lives. Particularly men with twelve-year-old daughters."

"And what is the silliness in *your* life?"

"Well…" Her hands lifted slightly, then fell back to her lap. "Maybe I've been a bit remiss in that area in my own life, lately."

He touched his finger to his mouth and pushed up.

Her head tilted. "You should get an A for effort," she assured, amused.

"And a D for results."

At that, she laughed.

And he felt the frown finally ease from his face. "You are an interesting woman, Helen."

"So you've said. I still am not entirely certain why."

"I find you…curious."

"Like a bug to be studied?"

He found he did wish to study her. For unfathomable reasons. Yes, she was a beautiful woman. But he had beautiful women available to him whenever he chose.

What was different about *this* woman?

The car pulled to a stop in the curving drive that fronted his daughter's boarding school. "There is a small garden if you would like to wait there," he told her when Akira opened the door.

"Yes, please."

The headmaster, a short, fastidious Briton named Mr. Hyde-Smith, had spotted the car and was hurrying toward them.

Mori spotted his daughter hanging back, near the heavy wooden gate that guarded the garden in the forecourt. Though it was dark, there was enough illumination from the lanterns to see that her appearance was, indeed, as shocking as Mr. Hyde-Smith had complained.

He headed toward the other man, wanting to avoid discussing his daughter's behavior in front of Helen. She had revealed herself to be a challenging opponent in their negotiations. For her to see that he was unable to control one small twelve-year-old girl would only weaken his position in her eyes.

Mr. Hyde-Smith bowed deeply as Mori reached him. "I didn't wish to disturb you, Taka-san, but as you can clearly see, Kimiko has broken our personal grooming requirements. Something must be done before the other students see her. Why, she could start a revolt!"

"Revolt is a strong word." Mori gestured to his daughter, who begrudgingly made her way to his side. She would not meet his gaze and he touched her hair that had been a gift from her mother—a deep brown silk— that was now as pink as bubble gum. "She can stay in her room until someone can be summoned to fix it."

"I'm sorry, Taka-san. We do not allow our students to make their hair vile colors, nor do we allow visible piercings or tattoos."

His mouth tightened. "Piercings?"

Kim rolled her eyes. "I don't have any piercings, Papa."

"The tattoo!" Mr. Hyde-Smith jogged Kimiko's arm and his daughter huffed and lifted it to her father's inspection.

The thing covered the entire length of her inner arm, from narrow wrist to inner elbow. An American flag.

He had last seen his daughter less than a week earlier.

Her arms then had still been untainted. "Go wait with Akira." His voice dropped.

Fortunately, she had the good sense not to argue.

When she was gone, Mori pinned his irritation on the headmaster. "What sort of supervision is occurring here that she not only has time to turn her entire head *pink,* but can have that thing applied to her arm?"

Mr. Hyde-Smith gulped a little. "It was a free day today, Taka-san. You were supplied the schedule at the beginning of the school term. We expect our pupils to monitor their own behavior, particularly when they reach Kimiko's age."

Mori knew what was coming even before the headmaster got there.

"Perhaps Kimiko would be happier in a different educational setting."

Mori wanted to gnash his teeth together. For the past year, the man had been hinting that his daughter would be better off elsewhere. "I will return my daughter in the morning," he told the man evenly. "Thank you for your trouble."

Mr. Hyde-Smith opened his mouth, but closed it again. He bowed. *"Domō arigatō gozaimasu,"* he murmured.

Mori was already heading back to the car.

Helen had remained seated inside, and he could see Kim leaning over, talking rapidly, her hands gesturing.

The gnawing headache settled in for a nice long visit. How long after a tattoo was given could it be removed?

Mori curtly told his daughter to stop disturbing Mrs. Hanson and to get into the vehicle.

She gave him a long look, but did as he bid.

Once they were inside, Akira drove away from the

small, prestigious boarding school. Kimiko was sitting between him and Helen. "This is Mrs. Hanson, Kimiko."

"Dōzo yoroshiku," his daughter mumbled.

"I'm pleased to meet you, too," Helen replied, in English. "Is that one of those stick-on tattoos?"

Kim held up the arm in question as if it were truly a thing to be admired. "I bought it in the marketplace this morning," she said.

"It is *temporary?*" His relief was so great he wanted to box her ears all over again.

"Yes," Kim said, as if he were dimwitted. "It washes off with soap."

"And will your hair wash back to its usual color?"

Her expression clearly told him it would not.

"You look like you have dipped your head in Day-Glo pink."

"It took three bottles," Kim said, then ducked her chin, evidently realizing that he was not as impressed with that fact as she.

"You have to dye it back."

His daughter remained stonily quiet.

"Why pink?" Helen asked, as if there were no tension congesting the vehicle at all.

"To match the dress I want to wear at my thirteenth birthday party."

"That is not for some time yet," Mori said evenly. "And long before then I expect my daughter to possess the color of hair with which she was born."

"When I move to America, I will make my hair every color of the rainbow." Kimiko looked up at Helen. "Maybe even gold as the sunrise. Could I have the color you have?"

"Well..." Helen's gaze flicked over his daughter's head for a moment, meeting his. "I'm afraid mine is pretty much what I was born with." She tugged the length of her thick ponytail over her shoulder. "It's darkened only a little since I was a girl. I always wanted to have beautiful, rich brown hair. Like a sable. But I never had the courage to try it."

"Changing it would be a waste." He eyed his daughter. "Now I have to find a professional to fix this mess. At this hour."

"I don't see why I have to change it at all."

"There are rules to be followed."

"It's a dumb rule."

He let out a sharp breath. He would not engage in an argument with his daughter in front of Helen. "Since you have delayed Mrs. Hanson's dinner long enough, you will join us for our meal. I will deal with you, afterward."

"It'll be even later then. To find a hairdresser, I mean." Helen's voice was cautious. "Perhaps we can take a rain check on dinner."

"Rain check?"

"A promise to do it another time."

Kimiko suddenly looked abashed. "Please, I do not wish to interrupt your meal, Mrs. Hanson. I am happy to do as my father requests."

"It is settled," Mori stated.

Helen was looking at his daughter. "And I am happy to have such a lovely girl join us for dinner."

Kimiko put a self-conscious hand to her hair.

It seemed that it took a woman to make her question whether or not her choice of hair color was wise. What her own *father* thought was another matter entirely.

Fortunately, they soon arrived at the Anderson hotel, and Mori escorted his companions to the restaurant. The maître d' greeted them all effusively and managed not to stare at Kimiko's head as he showed them to a table near the windows that overlooked the city lights.

Despite the excessively late hour, the restaurant was more than half full. Helen declined wine with a polite excuse, which surprised Mori, as did the order she made for a medium steak. Most of the women he knew—American or not—seemed to subsist on salads and little else.

He ordered a fruit tray for his daughter, who had already eaten her own dinner earlier, then his own preference—which happened to be nearly identical to Helen's.

The waiter disappeared as quietly as he'd appeared and Helen lightly touched Kimiko's colorful T-shirt. "Do you like fish?"

Her shirt was patterned with dozens of tropical fish. "I have an aquarium in my room at school," she said. Her English was only slightly accented. "Some day, my father may let me learn to scuba, so that I may see the fish without a cage."

"Scuba diving is a wonderful experience, but I haven't been in years. I've always loved watching fish in aquariums, though. There is something so peaceful about them."

"What kind of fish do you have?"

Helen shook her head. "None, I'm afraid."

"Papa, you must show Mrs. Hanson *your* fish." Like a Ping-Pong ball, Kimiko's attention bounced back and forth between the adults. "Bettas," she told Helen. "Very beautiful ones. My father has bred many of them. But the males have to be kept separate. They would fight."

"I've heard that." Her eyes were amused, but she did not seem to be bothered by Kimiko's rapid conversation. If anything, she appeared to be rapt.

The result of missing her own daughter's company at that age?

He decided he was speculating far too much about Helen's motives and her state of mind. "Kimi-chan," he murmured softly, silently warning her to cease her chatter.

His daughter's lashes swept down, hiding her expressive eyes. If it had not been for the yard-long skeins of pink hair streaming to the seat of her chair, she would have looked quite demure.

He knew better.

"Where have you been scuba diving?" he asked Helen.

Her fingers were slowly sliding up and down the stem of her water goblet. "Mostly the Caribbean. My husband used to enjoy it. When we first were married, we went often."

"Family holidays?"

Her fingers hesitated for just a moment, hardly long enough to be noticed. "Unfortunately, George's boys didn't accompany us. Have you been diving?"

He nodded.

"Papa prefers mountain climbing." Kimiko pressed her lips together, as if she had realized she may have been too free with information with their foreign guest.

"Kimiko is correct. I do prefer mountains to water. But, I have enjoyed many interludes beneath the surface."

Helen's smile widened. "What a lovely way of phrasing it."

What was lovely was the way her jadelike eyes sparkled when she smiled.

If she were merely a woman he had happened to meet, he would have had no qualms in pursuing the attraction. But she was in his country for professional reasons. That alone put her in a class where some men would feel perfectly comfortable in pressing their attentions on her, wanted or not.

He was not some men, however.

She was, for now, an opponent. When the acquisition of Hanson Media Group was complete, she would be a business associate—albeit one far removed from his center of operations here in Tokyo.

Attractive she was. Too wise to fall prey to it, he was, as well.

A phalanx of waiters arrived, bearing their array of dishes, and for a while, silence reigned over the table as Mori and his companions ate.

Kimiko finished her fruit in short order and, unable to overlook the tiredness in her eyes, he sent her up to his suite. "Wash the tattoo," he added, in case she had any ideas of leaving the colorful emblem in place.

He caught her rolling her eyes, but she went without debate.

Which left him alone with the puzzling and disturbing Mrs. Hanson.

"A few bottles of color from the drug store, and she'll be brunette once again."

"She does not stop to think about the consequences of her actions."

"She is twelve."

"More than old enough."

"When was the last time she was able to spend time with you?"

Too long. The thought had him frowning. "Why?"

"Maybe the pink hair is more a tactic to be with you than to satisfy her fashion urges."

He started to deny that, but stopped. They had already spoken too much of his family. "Kimiko is happy at school."

"Yes, I believe you mentioned that." Her voice was smooth. "It looked like a very old building. Beautifully maintained, but old. Did you, by any chance, attend there?"

"Yes."

She smiled softly. "Did you ever try some mischief to get beyond the walls?"

He and Shiguro had been terrors. But she need not know that. "No."

She merely chuckled, shaking her head. "And I never intentionally missed my ninth-grade English class, either."

He could easily imagine her as a young teenager. She had probably been the epitome of blond and carefree. "Do you wish to have a coffee?"

"I'd love one. But—" she looked regretful "—I must decline. If I have coffee at this hour, I'd be awake until dawn."

"You are tired." Though it did not show in her face. "I have kept you too long. Please forgive me."

"Not at all. It has been my pleasure."

"Akira will, of course, drive you to your hotel."

"It's not far. I can walk."

"That would be dangerous. A woman alone on the

streets at this time of night. If you will not allow Akira to drive you, then I will accompany you."

She stilled, her gaze measuring. "I am in the position of having to agree to your terms, aren't I? To do otherwise would be ungracious of me. Even though I am perfectly capable of finding my own way there."

"You have not been ungracious since we met." The truthful admission felt raw. He *much* preferred it when she did not speak her thoughts so freely. "If I were to acknowledge your capabilities, would you acknowledge that it would be safer for you to be transported to your hotel by someone I trust?"

Her head tilted slightly to one side. "Always the negotiator, Mr. Taka?"

"Earlier, it was Mori."

"So it was. *Mori.* I would be most happy to accept the offer of your driver," she capitulated. "Your daughter needs your attention tonight more than anyone. Thank you very much for the dinner. The food was delicious and the company delightful. Please tell your daughter I very much enjoyed meeting her."

Judging by Kimiko's equally rapt attention to Helen, the feeling had been mutual.

A disturbing fact, given his daughter's already inflated infatuation with Western ways.

"We will meet tomorrow."

"Around the conference table," she finished.

"Yes."

"I look forward to it." She bowed slightly, then walked out of the restaurant.

Watching her go, he knew he, also, was looking

Chapter Five

"What's this I hear about you and Mori Taka having dinner together last night?"

Helen paused, lifting her scone halfway to her mouth. How quickly word spread. "Good morning to you, too, Jack."

His lips tightened as he entered the living area of her suite. "You can't charm your way through the merger, Helen."

She gave him a long look. "I'm so flattered that you think I might try." Her tone was cooler than she intended. But, really, how long was she to be painted with the trophy-wife paint? "It was merely dinner, Jack."

"Mori doesn't *have* dinner with us, Helen."

"Well, he didn't with *you*," she agreed drily, which

was all she intended to say about the matter. "How is Samantha this morning?"

"Samantha is fine." The woman in question sailed into the room. "Jack, I hope you haven't been grilling Helen already. It's far too early for barbecue." Samantha leaned over and brushed her cheek against Helen's. "He's in a bad mood," she whispered sotto voce, before straightening again and sending her husband an impish smile.

No matter how irritated Jack might be with Helen, he still reacted to his wife's cheerfulness. The man was completely in love, and it pleased Helen in ways she could never adequately convey to her stepson. "Too much sake last night with Shiguro and the boys?"

Jack threw himself down on the couch opposite her. "We've got another week of meetings, at the very least, before we can sew this up. Then, what? Two or three months to make sure the transition goes smoothly?"

"Probably. Of course we'll be having the gala to celebrate the final signing well before that." She hoped that all of the boys would be in Tokyo for it. There would be *plenty* to celebrate, not least of which was the merger.

Samantha sat next to Jack, her hand smoothing over his thigh. "Jack found out this morning that one of his former law partners was appointed to the bench."

Understanding swept through Helen. "Things will work out, Jack. I know this has been frustrating for you, but, trust me. They *will* work out."

"Aren't you little Mary Sunshine."

"Jack," Samantha hushed.

"It's all right, Samantha." Helen took a small bite of her scone, but her appetite had waned. She leaned over the glass-topped coffee table and dragged her portfolio close enough to flip open.

Some of the time with Jack—most of the time—it was best for her to focus on facts.

She pulled out her latest sheet of notes, which she handed over to him. "Items I'd like to get cleared away with TAKA today."

He took the sheet, sitting forward.

Even with his dissatisfaction over being thrust into the management of his father's company, he wasn't going about it halfway. George had always been proud of Jack, though he'd been miserable at telling his eldest son that. Unfortunately, Helen was aware that expressing *her* pride in him wouldn't make up for his father's failings.

"You want to get back into the charitable giving again?"

"It has to be settled, Jack. If we don't do it now, we'll never get approval from the new board to continue a full match when the merger is complete. Not when TAKA will have a weighted presence."

Jack folded her notes and tucked it in his lapel pocket and stood. "Fine. I've got a conference call set up shortly with Evan about spinning off the radio division. We need to time it before the merger to keep the FCC happy. I'll see you before the meeting." He brushed his hand over his wife's hair and left just as abruptly as he'd arrived.

Helen looked over at Samantha. "It will be hard for him to stick out the transition period here."

"It isn't that he dislikes Tokyo," Samantha assured. "Quite the opposite, in fact."

"He misses his law practice."

The young woman nodded. "But, on a good note, we're considering finding a real place to live while we're here. Living in a hotel all that while doesn't appeal to either one of us. Having a place of our own, even temporarily, would be nice."

"I'm sure it would be. You and Jack haven't had a chance to really settle anywhere yet. There just hasn't been time with all the company issues in the way."

"Company issues that brought us back together in the first place." Samantha looked like the cat who got the cream as she grinned. "So…dinner with Mori Taka? What was that all about?"

"It was about nothing. His daughter was there, too."

"Introducing you to his family." Samantha nodded, slyly humorous. "Getting serious, already, eh?"

Even though Samantha was only teasing, Helen still felt her cheeks warming. "I'm sure he would have much preferred to keep his daughter far, far away from me."

"I don't believe that for a minute."

Helen just shook her head and waved her hand, trying to dismiss the matter. Too bad she couldn't dismiss it from her mind, however. Morito Taka was taking up much too much of her thoughts of late.

"He's a striking man." Samantha splayed her hand, studying her fingernails. "Intelligent, obviously. Rich, clearly. A woman could do worse."

Samantha *had* experienced much, much worse, at the hands of her first husband. "I'm *not* in the market for a man." Helen's voice was firm. "It hasn't even been a year since George died." But it had been far longer than that since she'd felt the interest of a man.

Perhaps that was why she couldn't get Mori out of her head. She'd been alone in her bed for too many years.

"Maybe you should be in the market," Samantha

countered, obviously not at all cowed by Helen's insistence. "There's no time frame on falling in love."

"Love?" Helen stood up so quickly she knocked her portfolio right onto the floor. "Believe me. The last person I would fall in love with is someone like Mori Taka. He's—"

Samantha had sat up, and was watching Helen closely. "He's…what? I know you're not going to say Japanese, because I won't believe for a second that the differences in your cultures would bother you in the least."

If anything, Helen found the differences as appealing as they were frustrating. But that was not the point. She picked up her portfolio and dropped it on the coffee table. "He's too much like George," she finally admitted.

"Jack's told me about his father," Samantha said slowly. "I don't see how the two are similar in the least, and I'm not talking about their ages."

She wished she hadn't said anything at all. Thinking about George was still painful, and not for the reasons Samantha would expect. Her friend believed that George had been the love of Helen's life. Helen had believed it, too, until the truth of George's feelings for her had capsized her life. "It doesn't matter, anyway. Once we finalize the merger, I doubt I'll have much interaction with Mori afterward. He'll be running TAKA from here, and I'll be back in the States."

"You still plan to be involved with the company, though."

Helen couldn't bring herself to lie, outright. Not when, with each passing day, she was wanting more and more to escape.

Ironic, given how many years she'd been disappointed in George's refusal to allow any involvement on her part in Hanson Media.

"Have you heard from Andrew or Delia? Do you know how she's feeling after the long flight back to Chicago?"

"Like she's ready to pop with the baby," Samantha answered. "Which she feels like despite international air travel. And she still has a few months to go. What are you not telling me, Helen?"

"Don't start imagining things." Helen pushed the tray of scones toward her. "Have you eaten yet?"

Her young friend made a face, but she dutifully picked up a scone and let the matter drop.

Helen was too wise to believe the subject would remain dropped, however. But for now, she was glad for the reprieve. "So, tell me. What kind of place do you and Jack want to find? A house? An apartment?"

Samantha smiled and began debating the merits of each. Helen focused her attention as best she could.

But it was hard, when her thoughts kept slipping to the unwanted appeal of Morito Taka.

Helen needn't have worried that she would not have all her wits about her that afternoon when facing off against Mori and his minions.

He wasn't there.

Shiguro offered no explanation over Mori's absence other than extending a profuse apology before taking Mori's seat at the head of the table and proceeding to be more obstreperous than ever before.

She actually found herself wishing that Mori *was* there, even though, up to now, he'd been a much more difficult prospect than Shiguro.

By the time they'd debated issues for two hours with no concessions whatsoever made on Shiguro's part, Helen had a raging headache.

Even Jack looked like he was on the verge of telling Shiguro to take a flying leap. When Shiguro actually retraced steps about the number of board positions that would be available to Hanson—a matter that had been firmly resolved already—Jack actually started to stand.

Helen saw the glint of satisfaction in Shiguro's eyes and without thought, cried out, distressed.

Heads swiveled her way as she swayed slightly, pressing a shaking hand to her cheek.

"Helen?" Jack looked concerned as he leaned over her. "What's wrong?"

"I'm so sorry." Her voice was weak. "I just felt faint. I—I'll be fine." She sat up a little straighter. "Please. Let's continue. Pay me no mind."

"Of course we will cease, Mrs. Hanson, if you are unwell." Evidently, Shiguro drew the line at taking advantage of a seemingly ill woman. He spoke sharply to the secretary taking the minutes, and the woman jumped up and scurried from the room. "I have sent for a physician."

Oh, Lord. This is what she got for acting without thought. "Please, I do not wish to cause an inconvenience. If I could just have a few minutes of rest."

Jack was eyeing her oddly. Naturally. The man was such a straight shooter.

Something she'd always tried to be, too. But desperate times called for desperate measures, and she'd been proving that for months now.

"She may rest in my office," Shiguro said.

It wasn't quite what Helen had hoped for, but beggars

couldn't be choosers. "Thank you very much for your kindness," she said weakly. "Jack, you'll help me, won't you?" She held her hands toward him.

He bent over her as he helped her out of her seat. She stumbled a little, resting her head against his shoulder, tossing in a pitiful moan for good measure.

"What are you doing?" he whispered as he half carried, half walked her toward the door.

"Hush."

He did, until they were closed in the relative privacy of Shiguro Taka's office.

Jack dumped her on a chair. "Have you lost your mind?"

Helen straightened her jacket. "Did you want to continue that farce of a meeting? There was no other way we could call a halt without—"

"—causing offense." He exhaled roughly. "I feel like we've taken two months' worth of work and tossed it out the damned window. What did you do with Mori last night, anyway, that he blew off the meeting today?"

She hated the defensiveness that swelled inside her. But she wasn't sure that she *hadn't* done something to set today's debacle in motion.

"I didn't *do* anything with him," she said truthfully. "You know as much about Mori's whereabouts today as I do." And getting angry served no good purpose. "I didn't know what else to do at the meeting, all right? If we were at home, I would have just said it was time to break, but you know that doesn't work here. Shiguro would take it as a sign of weakness on our part or a lack of respect for TAKA, or both. Either way, we'd be on the short end of the stick. But if they think I'm unwell, it's an excuse we can all forgive."

"You think they believed that little act of yours? You may be good at gaining the interest of wealthy men, Helen, but you are *no* actress."

She stomped down the pain inside her. She'd been acting for months and nobody had even known it. "It doesn't matter if they believed it or not, Jack. The point is, we're not going to let Shiguro call the shots, and he'll have gotten that message today, without having his nose rubbed in it."

"Games," Jack snapped. "It's playing games."

"Negotiations are a game," Helen said tiredly. Lord knew that George had taught her that quite well. "It's just one where the stakes involve more than a gold-plated trophy."

He raked his hand through his hair and paced the confines of Shiguro's office. It was surprisingly modest in size. "Now what do we do? Hang around for the next few hours waiting for them to get some doctor in here?"

"Don't worry. It'll only be a few minutes before they'll send someone in to check on us. We'll apologize most sincerely for the inconvenience I am causing and reschedule the sit-down. No harm, no foul."

He looked highly dissatisfied with the entire matter.

She couldn't blame him.

She wasn't feeling particularly satisfied with anything at the moment, either.

"If this merger falls through this late, Hanson won't be able to recover."

How well she knew that. "Hanson wouldn't have recovered if it had fallen through earlier, either, Jack."

He stared out the window, his hands shoved in his pockets. "Nice of my father to leave us with this mess, with no warning, no plans for how to save it all."

He'd had a plan, all right, Helen answered silently. Her headache seemed to worsen at the thought, and when Shiguro arrived with a physician in tow—one who spoke not one word of English—she didn't have to work very hard at feigning illness at all.

Helen sat there portraying "wan" and the men organized her return to her hotel, just as she'd known they would. And Jack, bless his heart, insisted on accompanying her, when Shiguro suggested resuming the meeting without her.

The man was not pleased, and as she spent the rest of the afternoon and evening alone in her hotel suite, going over the latest reports from Chicago, she couldn't help but wonder if Shiguro was suddenly manipulating things on his own accord, or if he'd been instructed to do so by the absent Mori.

She was sleeping when the phone rang.

She sat up with a start, blinking at the bright reading lamp beside the couch where she'd dozed off.

The clock read 2:00 a.m.

The phone rang again and she snatched it up, alarm in her voice. "Yes?"

"I heard you were feeling poorly."

The adrenaline pulsing through her abated slightly. Spread across the coffee table were the reports she'd been studying all evening.

They'd lulled her to sleep.

"Helen? Are you there?"

"I'm here. Mori? What are you calling at this hour for? Is there a problem?"

"You tell me."

She rubbed her hand down her face, trying to jump start her sluggish brain. "Where were you today?"

"My father-in-law died."

Shock provided more than the necessary spark to her brain. "Good heavens. I'm so sorry. Shiguro didn't say anything about it."

"I have heard reports from the meeting."

She could only guess what sort of slant they'd have if they'd been provided by his brother. And, she still wasn't convinced that Mori hadn't set up the entire thing—though it seemed oddly backhanded for a man who'd been perfectly upfront about his objections in the past.

"Are you all right?" she asked.

He was silent for a moment, as if her question surprised him. "Why would I not be?"

"Your wife's father?"

"It was…not unexpected. I did expect Shiguro to reschedule the meeting."

"You *did?*"

"He and my father believed it was more important to proceed."

The father with whom she knew Mori was often at odds. "I'm afraid we didn't get much accomplished."

"Because you were taken ill."

She covered her eyes with her hand, unable to form the lie. "Was it your decision to reduce our board positions from three to one?"

"The physician my brother provided. Was he helpful?"

In other words, no, the reduction hadn't been his

idea. If it had been his decision, he would have just said so. But he couldn't very well tell her that his brother had chosen to act without his approval.

"The doctor was very solicitous," she assured him. "Will you be needing to change the scheduled meetings, then? Because of your loss?"

"It would mean a delay of a week or longer."

Better a delay than to give Shiguro another opportunity to press his own agenda. "Then we will have a small delay," Helen said. "How is your daughter? Was she close to her grandfather?"

"She is back at school. Brown-haired again and broken-hearted over that more than the loss of a man she barely knew."

"Did your wife have siblings?"

"No. I am the closest family member. Sumiko's mother will need my assistance. I'll be in Takayama for several days."

"Of course. Mori, I am sorry. I'm glad you called."

"I should have waited until a more suitable hour to speak with you."

Why hadn't he? She badly wanted to ask, but refrained. "It's fine that you called me now."

"You were awake?"

"Well, no. But that's all right."

"I startled you."

He'd startled the life out of her. She couldn't get a call at such an hour anymore and not be reminded of the night she'd been phoned with the news that George had suffered a heart attack in his office. "A little," she admitted. "But I'm still glad that you called."

There was no denying the personal nature of his

doing so, though. "Is...is there anything I can do?" She knew the offer sounded ridiculous. She was a *gaijin*— a foreigner in his country. A person with whom he was associated only because of business purposes. Her question made about as much sense as him calling at such a late hour.

"No. Thank you."

She stared at her bare feet, hesitant to bid him the good-night that would be the sensible course. "So, Kimiko's hair is back to normal. Did the tat wash off?"

"Tat? Ah. The flag. Yes. It is gone. I am keeping you from your sleep," he said abruptly.

Since she'd met Mori, her sleep had been interrupted by him. He just wasn't privy to that fact. "Well, good night, then."

"*Kombanwa.*"

Helen hung up the phone. She didn't shut off the light and move to the bedroom, though, until she realized she was picturing Mori sitting on his end, staring at the phone the same way she'd been.

She hadn't brought very many personal items with her to Tokyo. Only clothes and accessories that she would need to get through the meetings with TAKA.

But she had brought her jewelry case.

Not the enormous locking monstrosity that George had once insisted she use to store the jewelry he liked her to wear when it wasn't in the safe, but a much smaller, simple wooden box. She lifted the lid.

Once, the box had contained only letters. Unsent letters that she'd written to her daughter. One every year since her birth.

Jenny had those letters now. Reading them had

helped to show her that she *hadn't* been unloved by her natural mother. That Helen hadn't shunted her off as a baby to the quickest taker just because it was the easiest solution for Helen.

Now, the jewelry box contained one narrow tray, partially filled with Helen's few necklaces and bracelets—and a dried leaf that she had kept for reasons that still escaped her.

But it wasn't any of those that drew Helen. It was the single folded sheet of paper beneath the tray.

She pulled it out. Unfolded the weighty stationery. Embossed at the top were George's initials.

Such familiar paper.

She'd given the stationery to him for their last anniversary, along with the gold pen she now used.

Quite a testament to one's marriage, wasn't it? A gift of personalized stationery and an engraved pen.

There had been no romantic evening for them to celebrate. Those had gone by the wayside years earlier, about the same time that George had told her he was not interested in having a baby with her, after all.

Back then, she'd blamed his decision on weariness over their failure to conceive, despite availing themselves of every conceivable technological advance in the area.

Now, Helen knew better when it came to George's motives. Their life together hadn't been based on love, at all. Not even from the beginning.

She unfolded the letter, her fingers smoothing along the creases.

Helen, it began. Not even a *dear,* or *my darling* to soften the words to come.

Helen,

I knew when we met that you'd make me an admirable wife. Beauty and intelligence is an appealing combination, so despite your modest beginnings, I knew your presence at my side would serve me well. The smartest thing I did was to marry you. I've watched you these years and you've never failed in meeting the purposes for which I chose you, whether it was charming my associates or hosting my friends. You were disappointed that I didn't publicly avail myself of your business acumen—the very thing that brought you into my world when you were nothing but a bright intern—but that didn't stop you from offering your thoughts all these years, even when they were unasked for. You have tenacity, Helen. And grit. I've always liked that about you. But now, you'll have to use those traits to undo what I've done. I always knew you'd outlive me, Helen. If you're reading this, then you'll know I was right in my thinking. Now I'm trusting you to take care of Hanson Media. You'll know what to do when the time comes.

It's all I have to give the boys, even though they never seemed much to want it. Maybe, as they get older, they'll be smarter than their old man, and put value where it is due.

Now, there's only one thing left for you to do, Helen.

Save the only thing that matters to me: Hanson Media.

It was signed, simply, *George.*

* * *

She could have recited the words by heart, so often had she made herself read it since she'd found it— sealed and addressed to her along with the pen he'd probably used to write it—waiting for her to discover in his personal papers at the office.

But the one word that the letter did not contain, the one word that would have meant the world to her, was the one he'd deliberately withheld.

Love.

George hadn't married her because he'd loved her. He'd married her for just exactly the things people had whispered.

Her youth.

Her looks.

Her intelligence, which he only wanted in evidence when they were in private.

It hadn't been love that prompted him to sweep her off her feet when she'd been a lonely intern with a fresh MBA. It had been his calculated mind that had seen which attributes would best serve his needs that had motivated their marriage. Unfortunately, Helen's love for him had blinded her to the truth. George hadn't really wanted her as a wife. She'd *been* a trophy because she'd allowed him to make her one. Yet he'd died trusting that she would be able to pull his company out of the fire.

She folded the letter and shoved it back in the box, flipping the lid closed. There were times she wished she'd burned the letter. Set a flame to it and watched it go up in smoke, just the way she'd felt the marriage she'd committed herself to out of *love* had gone up in smoke.

But she was what George said she was.

Tenacious.

Only now she had to prove to herself that she wasn't *only* what George had made of her—a wife chosen for her assets, rather than her heart.

If she had to work with TAKA in order to do that, she would. But once Hanson Media was secure again, joined at the hip with the juggernaut that TAKA was, she'd be happy never to think again of the man who hadn't loved her, after all, *or* his company.

Chapter Six

"You have a visitor, Helen."

Helen dragged her focus out of the month-ends and looked up. Her assistant, Sonia Townsley, stood in the doorway of her office. "I thought my only appointment was later."

"It is. Three-thirty with the broker who wants to list your house."

Helen pressed her fingers to her temple. She hadn't made up her mind yet what she would do with the house. But Darryl Waters was an old friend of George who'd been pushing for the listing. Since she was back in Chicago while Mori handled his father-in-law's matters, she'd agreed to discuss the matter with the broker, but only *discuss*. "Then who is here?"

Sonia slipped into the office, looking almost clandestine. "Morito Taka," she whispered.

Helen stared. *"What?"* She hadn't spoken with Mori since the night he'd called about his father-in-law, a week earlier. Because of the delay in negotiations, she'd decided to return to Chicago to attend to matters there while Jack and Samantha had remained in Tokyo.

"Not what. *Who.* Morito Taka." Sonia waggled her hand in front of her. "And if I might say so…holy cow. Wow." She collected herself when Helen just waited. "Everything is in such a mess up here that I put him in the conference room."

What would Mori be doing in Chicago? Unannounced, yet?

"Helen?"

She realized she was staring at the round fishbowl on the corner of her desk. The Betta seemed to be staring back at her as he slowly swished his brilliant blue tail. He'd arrived by courier a few days after her return.

A gift from Mori. A gift for which she worked hard at not placing too much importance. The Japanese were notorious for gift giving. The fish was nothing more than a polite courtesy. Nothing more significant than the collection of funky hair ornaments that she'd sent to him for Kimiko.

"The conference room is fine," she said.

"He'll want a tour, I suppose. I can give the departments a heads-up."

"Of course. Right. Good idea." She stood and smoothed back her hair as Sonia headed to the door. "No. Wait."

Her assistant stopped, her eyebrows lifted. "Yes?"

Why would he make such an unprecedented visit? Was it another attempt to call off the merger?

Just because the final negotiations had been temporarily halted, did that mean he wanted to halt them permanently?

She looked at the fish, her mind teeming. Mori the man. Mori the opposition. Which was real? Which did she trust?

She closed her eyes for a moment, shutting out the sight of the exquisite fish. The debate going on inside her head wasn't so easily avoided.

"Don't call anyone," she said. "Mr. Taka will have his tour. There's nothing at Hanson that isn't up to snuff." She tugged the hem of her jacket and headed out the door. "Don't worry, Sonia," she assured. "Go back to what you were doing. And call Darryl for me to reschedule."

"Shouldn't I call Evan or Andrew? Or David?"

"There's nothing to call them about," Helen said. "If Mori thinks he's going to find us less than prepared, he's wrong. Period."

Sonia looked uneasy, but she nodded, and Helen made her way to the conference room.

Despite the several days since she'd last seen Mori in Tokyo, the sight of him still had her catching her breath. He was standing at the window, looking out.

She moistened her lips, wishing she'd taken a few minutes just to freshen her lipstick, then was annoyed at her own insecure vanity.

She straightened her shoulders and entered the room. "Mori. This is a surprise."

He turned. As always, he wore a suit. This one was a dove gray that ought to have given him a more approachable look than his typical black. It didn't. He was as unreasonably attractive as ever, too.

"Not an unwelcome surprise, I hope," he replied smoothly.

"Of course not." She crossed the carpet toward him, hand extended, which he shook. Thankfully, the disturbing contact was brief. "Quite the opposite," she assured, hoping she wasn't telling a blatant lie. "It will be a pleasure to finally show you our shop here."

"The reports from my associates who have been here have always been most complimentary." His voice was so diplomatic she had the sudden urge to laugh. She knew good and well that his associates had returned to him every nitpicking detail about the Chicago office in order to increase TAKA's bargaining power and decrease Hanson's.

"Well, you've seen the view—" she nodded her head toward the bank of windows "—so, shall we see the rest?"

"You have the time?"

"Actually, no," she admitted wryly. "I'm in the middle of pulling together month-ends for a certain CEO."

His lips lifted in one of his rare smiles. "A tyrant?"

At that, she did laugh. Softly. The man definitely had a way of surprising her. "An excellent negotiator," she corrected. "We'll start here on this floor and work our way down."

"And will you show me every nook and cranny?"

"Every dusty corner," she assured lightly, and exited the room ahead of him.

She was painfully aware of the warmth of him as he followed her, which was ridiculous given the circumspect distance he maintained between them.

They made their way along the corridor, and Helen pointed out each office, stopping to make introductions along the way. She knew it was unaccustomed behavior for him—he negotiated deals at the highest level. He wasn't one to take note of every employee under the roof.

But Helen was. That was the way Hanson Media worked now, and Mori might as well learn that fact, for good or bad. And, she was relieved to see, nobody quailed at meeting the big man himself. To a one, her staff members were dignified, professional and welcoming. Unfortunately, David, George's younger brother, who was in charge of PR; and Evan, George's middle son, were both out of the office at meetings. "Andrew," she told Mori, as they passed his empty office, "is with his wife, Delia. Do you remember her from Richard and Jenny's wedding?"

"Yes. She is carrying your first grandchild."

She hesitated only momentarily, before answering with a smooth smile. The truth was, she didn't have any expectations that Andrew would want his and Delia's child to think of her as a grandparent.

She was just grateful that she was truly happy for Delia, who—at thirty-seven—was carrying a baby when at the same age, Helen had been unable to conceive. She'd been somewhat afraid that she'd be envious of her. Instead, she'd only felt pleasure and anticipation.

Thank goodness.

But that didn't mean Helen was certain that *she* was ready to be thought of as a grandparent, either.

They finished exploring the floor and then returned to her office. Mori glanced around, not seeming particularly interested in the furnishings or the view beyond

the sparkling windows. He bent slightly and looked at
the fishbowl, however.

Helen had not only sent him a written thank-you for
the gift, she'd personally calle,d as well. "The fish was
a very thoughtful gift," she said. "Again, I thank you."

"You did not tell me he was your officemate."

"Well, I'm here more than I am at home. Captain
Nemo would get lonely at home."

"Captain Nemo?"

"From *Twenty Thousand Leagues Under the Sea.*
The book."

He straightened. "Yes. I know it."

She folded her hands together, hoping she hadn't in-
advertently insulted him. "Shall I show you the rest of
our offices? Do you have time constraints?" She ought
to have asked that earlier. The man could have a dozen
reasons for being in the States that did not concern
Hanson Media Group in the least. "Perhaps Evan and
David will be able to make a late lunch with us."

"My time is yours."

A few weeks earlier and she would have found that
idea daunting. Now she found it…disturbingly appealing. "All right, then. Back to seeing those nooks and
crannies." She headed out of her office. "Sonia, check
David's and Evan's schedules and see if we can't get in
somewhere for lunch."

Her assistant nodded. "Will do."

Satisfied, Helen headed toward the elevator. Mori
touched her elbow as they got on, just a slight grazing
of his fingertips, and she stopped, looking up at him.

His faint crows feet crinkled. "I find I have missed
our conversations."

She couldn't have moved then if a train had been bearing down on her. "I'm not sure if you're pulling my leg, or not."

He glanced down. "Lovely though they are, I must refrain."

The laughter rose in her throat before she could stop it. If a man were to say such a thing to a woman in the workplace nowadays, he'd be accused of harassment. "How fortunate for me," she returned humorously and managed to keep herself from smoothing a self-conscious hand down her skirt.

The fact of the matter was, she wasn't altogether sure she wouldn't like his hands on her legs. Very much.

And wasn't that quite the admission standing in her husband's office building?

George is gone.

She banished the whispered reminder from her thoughts and left the elevator when the doors opened. Mori followed.

Was he looking at her legs?

Stop thinking like a schoolgirl.

She walked a little more quickly, heading toward the print division. His long legs easily kept pace beside her. "When did you arrive in the U.S.?"

"This morning."

She slowed, glancing up at him. "Aren't you tired?"

"Not particularly."

She found the trip between Tokyo and Chicago exhausting.

"I am almost a day younger here, after all," he continued. "Is that not the ultimate quest of the Americans? To find their youth?"

"But you'll regain the day when you return home," Helen reminded. "And I might miss the days when I didn't…creak quite so much when I get up in the morning, but I can't say returning to *my* youth is all that appealing."

She pushed through the double doorway and entered a cacophony of voices and computer keys. "Speaking of youth, however, how is your daughter?"

"Still brown-haired. She sends me e-mail photos of herself wearing the hair decorations you sent. She is most pleased with them. I will forward a few to you if you would like to see them."

Helen managed not to smile too widely as she paused inside the doorway. "I would love to. I'm glad she is enjoying them. She was delightful, even with the pink 'do.'"

"She looked…common."

"She's only experimenting, Mori. She struck me as incredibly bright and creative."

"She can be bright and creative when she is in university. Until then, she needs to focus on her studies."

"Never underestimate the importance of education," Helen agreed. It had taken her longer than usual to obtain hers, but she'd finally put herself through college working nearly any job she could get to pay for her MBA.

And then she'd met George and her career aspirations had taken a backseat.

She lifted her arms, encompassing the pack of cubicles and desks and the people who worked at them.

"The heart of the newspaper," she said, raising her voice a little. "This is where Hanson Media Group all began." She continued her stint as tour guide, entering the fray, making introductions and briefly describing each person's role.

It had taken her nights of study to learn all the names and responsibilities. But it had been well worth it when she'd been able to knowledgably discuss the staff that first day after George's will had put her in charge.

Hanson had endured heavy layoffs shortly after Jack had come on board and discovered the seriousness of his father's mismanagement. By knowing the people who remained, Helen had been able to earn their otherwise reluctant trust.

There was still an element of fear underriding most everyone who worked at Hanson Media, but it didn't have the crews heading for the nearest porthole, ready to desert a sinking ship. They were sticking tight and well, not certain how the entire merger would work out, but willing to wait and give it a chance.

Mori, she noticed as they finally made their way through the other divisions—even radio, which he didn't have to show an interest in since that had to be separated from Hanson Media Group before they could become part of a foreign company—seemed much more approachable than he did walking the corridors of his own castle.

He just smiled faintly when she dared comment on it once they returned to her office. He'd seated himself in one of the side chairs around the small round table in her office. "If I were to engage in conversation with the salary men, word would quickly spread that I had lost my sanity. I would no longer have their respect."

Sonia popped her head in. "David can meet you at Benny's at two. I haven't been able to reach Evan. I've left a message for him."

"Thanks, Sonia."

Her assistant smiled and disappeared again, closing the door behind her.

Helen wished Sonia hadn't done that. It seemed to add too much privacy to her meeting with Mori. So, she busied herself pouring them both glasses of water from the pitcher Sonia had placed on the table while they'd been touring the building. "How is your mother-in-law doing?"

"She is well. She is visiting my mother's home for a few days."

"Your two families are close, then? They live some distance from each other, don't they?"

"Hai." His long fingers slowly circled the glass, but he did not lift it. "The Yamamoto and Taka families were the oldest in Nesutotaka. My mother and Sumiko's mother were like sisters growing up. Sumiko's mother moved away when she married, however. But they still remained friends."

"And they liked the idea of their children marrying?"

"It was not a sentimental decision," Mori explained. "Sumiko's lineage was desirable to my father's family. TAKA had provided my family with great wealth, but it is the Yamamoto family that once had ties to the emperor. My mother and father's marriage was decided upon for similar reasons. Each generation has made an advantageous match."

"And you think your daughter should do the same, when she's older."

"You have that look of disapproval in your eyes, Helen."

She looked down at her hands. She was holding her glass in the same way that Mori was. Only a few inches separated their knuckles. "People, even Americans, marry for all sorts of reasons. But I'm old-fashioned enough to wish everyone would marry only for love."

"I think that is more a romantic belief than an old-fashioned one. Even Americans have had arranged marriages, and not so many generations ago."

She couldn't dispute the truth of that. "Well, these days marriage here is so easily entered and exited that I think it takes a deep emotional commitment to make it last. And if the people don't care about making it last, then what is the point of marrying in the first place?"

She looked up to find him watching her with that mesmerizing stare of his, and felt her cheeks heat. She laughed lightly. "And if that isn't getting away from the purpose of your visit, I don't know what is."

"You had this deep emotional commitment to your late husband?"

She inhaled a little. "I did."

His eyes narrowed a little and she knew he'd caught her unconscious emphasis of "I." But he let the matter pass without comment, for which she was profoundly grateful. "The purpose for my visit was not to tour Hanson," he said. "Though I did find it enlightening."

Enlightening? She stifled her wariness over that particular statement. "Then what is the reason you're here?"

"To offer you my apology."

Her heart dove right down to her toes. She couldn't have drawn a breath if she'd been a red flag waved in front of a bull's nose. "You're calling off the merger."

His eyebrows shot together. "You have gone as pale as moonlight. Drink your water."

If she drank, she'd vomit. All these months of maneuvering, of planning, negotiating, of sleepless nights and endless days had been for naught.

She'd failed.

He made a sound under his breath and wrapped his hand around hers on the glass, lifting it toward her mouth. "Drink," he ordered. "I am not, as you say, *calling off* anything. The acquisition is proceeding."

There was an odd buzzing sound inside her head. Water filled her mouth and she swallowed before it spilled over her chin. "Merger," she mumbled.

His lips twitched. "Better." He lowered their hands and set the glass on the table. "Do not faint. I would not know what to do with you."

"I have the feeling you *always* know what to do," she murmured. She realized his hand was still covering hers, and his fingers felt warm and…comforting.

She didn't want comforting. She wanted the merger inked so maybe her life would lose the nightmarish tinge it had developed. "What do you mean by apologizing, then? You've done nothing that requires one." Certainly not something that would necessitate a trip from Japan to offer it.

"My father does not wish for TAKA to become involved with American business," he said. "He strongly disapproves of it."

"Your father is no longer CEO of TAKA, though. You are." If Yukio Taka had still been in control, she *never* would have gone to TAKA.

"It is not our nature to dishonor one's father."

"Well, I can certainly understand that. And I respect that. But I still don't—"

"You will let me continue?"

She clamped her lips shut and nodded.

He sighed a little. "My father met with Shiguro on the day that I was unable to attend our scheduled meeting."

"When your father-in-law passed away."

"*Hai*. That day. My father convinced Shiguro to try to renegotiate some of our previously approved items."

"The number of board seats."

"*Hai*. Shiguro, he is a good man. A good…son. I regret that his good intentions to our father were insulting to you and your associates. Shiguro offered to come here himself, as he should. But it is I who is ultimately to blame."

"You weren't responsible for what your brother decided to do, Mori."

"Everything that occurs in the house of TAKA is my responsibility. I wish to assure you that the Hanson seats are unchanged."

"Well. I'm relieved to know that we won't have to battle *that* out again. It was difficult enough in the first place. Of course, I accept your apology."

"Though you find it unnecessary."

His fingers were more tanned than hers, the backs of his hands slightly dusted with hair.

Masculine hands. Strong hands.

She'd seen him casually wield the sword in his hotel suite. Would his hand be as deft without a weapon?

She swallowed.

"Perhaps unnecessary, but welcome all the same," she assured, casually pulling her hand free of his by reaching for the pitcher and refilling the glass. "It is reassuring to have confirmation that Shiguro's actions that day hadn't been at your request."

"I do not force my decisions through other parties."

"No, you don't. You say right up front that something is or isn't acceptable. It's very honest. I admire that."

"Honesty isn't always a part of business."

She shook her head. "Or life." Then, because that seemed too dreary altogether, she looked at her watch. "We should go if we're going to catch David at the restaurant. It's a popular haunt of Hanson people, just a few blocks from here, if you don't mind walking?"

"No, I do not mind."

She retrieved her purse from the drawer in the desk and after confirming that Sonia had been able to change Helen's appointment with the real estate broker, she and Mori left the building.

It was a particularly stunning day outside, just breezy enough to lend a coolness to the day, and a hint of approaching autumn weather. As they walked, Helen pointed out directions for some of the more famous landmarks—the Sears tower, the Hancock Building— and before she knew it, they were entering the dark, cavelike entrance to Benny's. Several steps down, the light moderated some, and the jazz trio playing in the corner could be heard.

It was quite unlike any place that TAKA had hosted them at in Tokyo and she couldn't help but wonder what Mori's reaction would be. She spotted David already seated, and wove her way through the closely set tables to him.

Her brother-in-law stood as she approached and stuck out his hand to Mori as she made the introductions. "David was George's younger brother," she told him, even though Mori would certainly be aware of the relationship. "Hanson's PR department is incredible and it's all because of David."

"Helen gives me too much credit," David said easily. "We have a great public relations department because we have a great group of people who make it so."

They sat and a waitress sidled by, depositing a tray of warm rolls and cold crudités in the center of their table. "Drinks?"

"Iced tea for me," Helen said. David and Mori both nodded and the waitress disappeared again.

"So, Mr. Taka, what prompted your visit to Chicago?" David's question was congenial, but she certainly knew what he had to be thinking beneath it. The same thing she'd been afraid of.

"Mostly social," Mori told him and his gaze was on Helen as he said it.

Her mouth went a little dry and she wished the waitress would hurry with the iced tea.

"Well, if you want to see anything of the city, Helen's your girl. She knows the place like the back of her hand."

"Does she?" A faint smile played around Mori's sharply carved lips. "How…convenient for me."

"David is too modest," Helen countered. "He's lived here longer than I have."

"Maybe," David conceded, "but I wouldn't make as entertaining a guide as you. Plus, if you get tired of the typical tourist attractions, you might enjoy seeing the house. George and Helen's place. It's considered one of the finest properties in the city."

Helen found her gaze trapped by Mori's. "Then I must not miss seeing Helen's place," he stated.

Forget dry-mouthed. She was dying, purely and simply.

From somewhere, however, she dredged up an agreeable nod. "I would be pleased to show you my home, Mori."

And then his smile widened, and she wasn't sure that receiving an invitation to her home hadn't been his intention, all along.

But why?

Hosting business associates at their place had been one of the things George had evidently married her for. She'd done it often and done it well.

So why did the idea of Mori Taka being under her roof send every nerve she possessed into a fit of the screaming meemies?

Chapter Seven

Helen's shrieking nervousness was still well in play later that evening as she put the finishing touches on the table.

She'd set two place settings at one end of the mile-long dining table. On any given day, the table could seat twenty, and while Helen might have felt safer putting Mori at one end and her at the other, she did realize that doing so would look as infantile as it felt.

It's only a business dinner.

She kept telling herself that while she straightened the blown glass vase containing a tight bouquet of Sterling roses. It's only a business dinner. Only.

"Mrs. Hanson?" Gertrude, the housekeeper, who was the only staff person whom Helen had kept on, spoke from the dining room entrance. "I've selected a few wines from the cellar for your dinner. Would you like to look them over?"

Helen shook her head. Gertrude had worked for George even before their marriage. Helen hadn't had the heart to suggest she retire, and these days, it was only the two of them who floated around the enormous house. Helen had left it up to Gertrude to hire a cleaning service to help her, and had been grateful when the older woman finally, grudgingly, allowed a strictly supervised crew to come in monthly and do the "heavy work" as Gertrude called it. "I'm sure whatever you chose will be perfect."

Gertrude hesitated a little, her light blue gaze somewhat curious. "This *is* a business dinner?"

"Yes." Helen turned the vase an inch.

"For two."

Another quarter inch. "Yes."

Gertrude sniffed a little and came more fully into the room. "Pardon me for saying so, Mrs. Hanson, but it *is* okay for you to have a date."

Helen jerked and stared at Gertrude. "Excuse me?"

"You're a young woman. You shouldn't be alone."

Her cheeks flushed. "I don't feel all that young, I'm afraid."

"Oh, garbage." Gertrude patted her ample hips. "*I* am not all that young, and even I have a gentleman caller from time to time."

Helen raised her eyebrows.

"Now, don't look so surprised, Mrs. Hanson. I'm a woman, after all."

"Yes, you are, Gertrude. And one I'd be lost without." She looked at the table. "But this really *is* a business dinner."

Gertrude looked regretful. "Well, all right. If that's the case, then I really should stay to serve and clean up after."

"No, you shouldn't. All I have to do is pull things out of the oven and fridge because you're so organized. Go." She smiled. "Call up your gentleman friend and go wild."

"You go ahead and laugh," Gertrude replied blandly, "but you just might be surprised what a woman my age can get up to."

Helen chuckled. "I'm not laughing at you, my friend. You give me hope."

Gertrude patted Helen's shoulder. "Go put on something pretty."

Helen looked down at her clothing. "What's wrong with this?"

"Even if it is a business dinner, you don't have to wear an iron gray suit."

"You make it sound like I look like a prison matron," Helen murmured. "This is a designer suit."

"I suppose I could scare up some handcuffs and a baton for you," Gertrude replied, "but something a little softer might be more appealing, fancy designer name or not."

The doorbell chimed softly.

And for all of Helen's insistence that this dinner was strictly business, she froze.

Gertrude, bless her soul, refrained from saying "I told you so," but her arch expression conveyed it anyway. "Skedaddle up those stairs to your room. I'll let in your guest and show him into the library. Cozier there than the living room, don't you think?"

Helen didn't know what to think. She just went up the stairs at a rapid clip, hearing Gertrude head to the door behind her.

In her closet, Helen stared at the racks of clothing. What would she wear? She grabbed a hanger.

A skirt that left *way* too much of her thighs bare? No. That was from the George days.

She tossed the hanger aside and grabbed another.

Suits, suits, suits. She owned dozens of them. Found them to be her safety net in fashion, and had ever since she buried her husband along with his desire to see her in the latest fad, even when *she* had felt ludicrous wearing such revealing items.

Her heart was thudding in her chest, and she could actually feel herself beginning to perspire.

"Get a grip, Helen."

She turned away from the side of her closet filled with suits, and the side still filled with her George-days wardrobe. Jeans were much too casual, as were her plethora of capris and workout garments.

From downstairs she could hear the faint sound of the heavy front door closing and imagined Mori walking through her home, escorted by Gertrude to the library. There wasn't a fire burning in the fireplace down there, but it still would offer a decidedly intimate feel for Mori.

Why hadn't she told Gertrude to put him in the living room?

She groaned and grabbed a sleeveless white sweater and a pair of loose silk slacks. In seconds, she'd replaced the iron maiden. She hurried out of her room, dashing down the stairs and practically running to the library.

She stopped outside the arched doorway and, smoothing back her ponytail, drew in a long breath, grabbed composure with a desperate grip and entered the room. "Mori, I'm so sorry to keep you waiting."

He wasn't wearing a suit, either, she thought inconsequentially. A thin cashmere sweater the color of nutmeg covered his chest and chocolate brown slacks completed the look.

Very chic.

Very…handsome.

Very…un-Mori.

The man had probably been born in a suit. How could she continue convincing herself they were having dinner in her home for purely business reasons when the man didn't even have the decency to dress for the occasion?

"You did not keep me waiting," he said, interrupting the flow of insanity inside her brain. "I was studying your book collection. It is very eclectic."

"Most of it was George's."

He pulled out a narrow leather-bound volume. "Emily Dickinson?"

"Not all of the collection was George's," she qualified.

He smiled faintly and slid the book back into place.

Her palms felt moist. She curled them over the back of the upholstered love seat that faced the stone fireplace. "Did you settle in to your hotel all right?"

"Yes." His gaze continued traveling over the room, and finally settled on her.

She should say something. She was a grown woman. A sophisticated woman. Everyone said so.

So why couldn't she find a single coherent thought inside her entire stupid head?

"Thirsty?" she blurted. "I mean, would you like a drink?"

"Beer, if you have it."

She pressed the tip of her tongue against the inside of her teeth. "Have a seat. I'll be right with you."

He nodded, but turned back to the towering shelves filled with books. As soon as she saw him pulling one out, she made herself move sedately from the room.

Good as her word, Gertrude had already departed. Probably because she'd taken one look at the very sexy Mori Taka and decided that she could be absent for *this* particular business dinner. Helen yanked open the stainless steel refrigerator door and crouched down, studying the contents, hoping there would be a beer or two lurking in the cavernous confines.

There wasn't.

Her breath hissing between her teeth, she quietly darted through the house and into George's home office. Sure enough, there were still bottles in the small refrigerator hidden in the wall. She grabbed a few and ran back to the kitchen where she poured herself a short, squat glass of ice water. She set everything on a silver tray, added a bottle opener and a pilsner glass from the cupboard and carried it back to the library.

He was sitting on the love seat.

Somehow, his choice made her uneasy.

Not uneasy in a fearful way, but uneasy in a woman-man sort of way.

She really was losing her mind.

She smiled at him and set the tray on the table next to the love seat. There was no coffee table between it and the fireplace; only an exotically thick off-white Flokati rug covered the carpet.

There were three other chairs near the love seat and

she chose the closest one to him before opening the beer to pour into his glass. "I hope import is okay." She handed it to him.

He looked amused as he reached over and wrapped his hand around the tall, skinny beer bottle she still held. "It is a Japanese beer. To me, it is not an import."

She laughed and shook her head at herself. *"Sumi-masen."*

He handed her the remaining glass and lifted his in a toast. *"Kampai."*

She took the glass from him, grateful that she'd stuck with water and not anything alcoholic. Her head was already swimming enough. "Cheers."

They drank.

Then, not wanting another awkward silence to descend between them, Helen stood. "Please excuse me. I just need to check the oven for a moment. I hope you like chicken." She didn't say it out of courtesy. She was suddenly very aware that during the dinner they'd had that one night, he'd ordered beef.

"I do."

She was appalled at the relief that rolled through her. "I'll be right back."

He smiled faintly.

She took off, rolling her eyes at herself. The man was clearly amused at her.

A fine thing for someone she wanted—needed—to have some measure of respect for her when it came to the bargaining table.

The chicken was perfectly fine when Helen peeked in the oven. How could it not be, with Gertrude having prepared it, and the state-of-the-art oven that shut itself off at the precise time, merely keeping the contents at an optimal temperature?

"It smells good."

She slammed the oven door shut and turned. "I…yes. It does. We can thank Gertrude Singer for that. My… um, my housekeeper. And cook, and everything else I need, pretty much."

"But you say you like to cook?"

"I do. But, somehow, I thought homemade pizza might not be your cup of tea."

He set his beer on the granite island that consumed the center portion of the window-lined kitchen. "I do not prefer anchovies on my pizza, but otherwise, Kimiko keeps me well acquainted when she is with me." He pulled out one of the iron-legged barstools on the far side of the island and leaned against it. "You are nervous."

And thank you for pointing it out. "Not at all."

He tilted his head slightly, looking down at the floor. "You have no shoes."

She looked down.

Lord. She'd forgotten to put on shoes.

"Perhaps I don't wear street shoes in my home."

"I doubt that is your custom here," he said wryly.

She wanted to curl her bare toes against the slate tile. "I…forgot," she admitted. "It had nothing to do with nervousness. Just rushing."

If she were Pinocchio, her nose would be a foot long by now.

"Here. Drink."

She realized he'd also brought in her glass of water. "Thank you." She took it and swallowed it down, realizing belatedly that he probably assumed she'd just chugged a half-full glass of vodka or something. Well, that was too bad. At every meeting they'd had in Japan involving the dinner hour, alcohol had flowed freely, even though she'd rarely drunk much more than appearances required.

She just didn't have a head for it.

"Dinner is ready, if you'd like to eat now. Or perhaps you'd like me to show you around the house?" That was, supposedly, the excuse for this tête-à-tête. For him to see the marvel that was George Hanson's abode.

"You can give me the tour after."

"It will be my pleasure. The dining room is this way." She started from the kitchen, only stopping once she reached the formal dining room and held out her arm. "Please. Have a seat."

He looked up at the high frescoed ceiling then around the large room. "An impressive room."

"That seems to be the impression most people have."

"And you?"

She tried looking at the room with fresh eyes. "It is impressive. And large. And—" she rocked her head from side to side "—and...large."

"Very large."

She felt a smile budding around her lips—a real smile. "Well. We *could* eat in the kitchen."

"Would that scandalize you?"

Surprisingly, her grin broke right out at that. "Mori, if you haven't realized it yet, scandal is becoming second nature to me." Then she held her breath, because, though she was *almost* getting to the point where she could speak lightly of painful things that had been mucked about in the press about her, she wasn't at all certain he would feel the same.

But a dimple slowly appeared in his cheek as he smiled. "The kitchen it shall be." Suiting words to action, he crossed to the table and deftly stacked the plates.

She hurried after him, picking up the flatware and linens and stemware.

They reset their table at one end of the island. Mori disappeared for a moment while she was busy serving up the roast chicken and setting out side dishes.

She was just finishing when Mori returned. He wasn't carrying the foot-high vase, but he was carrying one of the roses.

She set the wine Gertrude had chosen on the counter and eyed the flower. The barely unfurled blossom looked delicate and silvery against his fingers.

Then he handed her the rose. "If you would please hold this?"

She took it, watching curiously as he picked up his beer bottle. He looked very serious then as he shook out his ivory linen napkin, made a fold or two, followed by a few deft twists that she could barely follow, and swaddled the bottle in ivory linen.

The finished product looked like a flower itself, and then he took the rose from her and dropped the stem into the center of his creation.

She slipped onto one of the stools. "Well, my goodness. Does the TAKA board know what highly developed skills you're hiding?"

"You would not be so impressed if you saw what Shiguro can do with a cherry stem."

It took her a bare moment longer than it should

have to realize he was joking because his expression was so deadpan.

She smiled and pointed at him with a stern finger. "You're a tough one, Mr. Taka. But I know your secret now. You *do* have a sense of humor."

"Do not let my senior management hear that."

She pressed her lips together and mimicked twisting the key. "The secret will go with me to my grave."

He lifted the wine bottle and filled their glasses. "However, now that you know my secret, you must share with me yours, or we shall be on uneven footing again when next the lawyers crack their whips."

"Ah." She sipped her wine, watching him over the rim of her glass. The man was too attractive by far and drinking wine would only lower her defenses against him. "All of my secrets have been splashed about already. Part and parcel of that scandal thing, you know."

"That is not an answer."

"I kind of thought it was," she countered lightly and set down the wine to reach for the carving knife. "Light or dark?"

"Light."

She quickly carved a slice of succulent chicken and slid it on his plate, then repeated the process for herself.

"You are delaying."

She lifted her eyebrow. "A woman should never divulge her secrets so easily."

"Negotiation." He nodded, seemingly thoughtful. "You like the negotiation as much as you do the end result."

She thought of some of the endlessly tedious meetings she'd endured with TAKA. "Not *every* step of the negotiation."

"Still, you delay."

She pressed her lips together and shot him a long look, which he ignored as he took over serving duty and filled her plate with more food. "I won't be able to eat all of that," she finally said.

"Negotiation is good for the appetite."

She smiled sweetly. "You're an amazingly annoying man, do you know that?"

"So I have been told. The secret?"

She took a fortifying sip of wine. "All right. Sometimes I wish I could chuck all of the business and run away to hide. Just for a few days." To forget she was a widow, that she was fighting tooth and nail to prove her own worth. "Now, see? That was much more *secret* than you expected."

"This is why I go to my home in Nesutotaka. To escape."

"You need to escape? I thought you thrived on the pressure of heading up TAKA."

"Sometimes a man just wants to be a man." His hooded gaze no longer seemed amused as he focused it on her face. "Just as a woman simply wants to be a woman."

Her mouth went dry again and she doused it with another fair dose of the grape. Her half glass was down to a fourth. "And when you escape, do you work in your garden? Mountain climb?"

"You remember our conversation that day."

"I remember everything," she murmured.

"And forgive nothing?"

She hesitated, caught by the question. "No. I'd like to think I forgive."

"Others or yourself?"

The conversation was becoming far too personal for comfort. What would Mori Taka know about matters so intimate to her? Was he taking a shot in the dark, or did her failures show that clearly on her face and in her life?

So she just smiled confidently and picked up the wine bottle. "More?"

He nudged his empty glass within reaching distance of her pour, yet when she finished and set down the bottle, he didn't pick up his glass.

Instead, he caught her hand in midair.

She stilled, looking at his hand on hers. His fingers were warm as he tilted her hand. The diamond setting on her wedding band had turned slightly on her finger and he pressed his thumb against it, moving it until the ring was centered once more. The diamond caught the light and sent gleaming prisms dancing around them.

"You do not eat enough," he said. His thumb nudged the setting once more. The prisms died as the ring slid much too easily around her finger. "What is it you worry about?"

She managed a light laugh and tugged her hand free of his. "Well, I won't worry that my Pilates trainer is ineffective."

"Pilates?"

"It's a type of exercise."

"You need less Pilates, and more food."

"Gosh. Thanks, Mori. Every woman wants to be told she's too skinny. It's right up there with being told she's too heavy."

His slashing eyebrows pulled together over his nose. "I am not wishing to tell you these things. I am expressing concern."

"You have no reason to be concerned," she assured, but her voice didn't hold the ring of authority she'd have preferred. "I'm not suffering from consumption. I'll summon strength enough to celebrate the merger when it's complete, believe me."

"As I told you before, not everything is about business."

She needed to remind him of her response to that, but for some reason she just didn't have the energy to do so. She reached for her wineglass only to realize it was empty. Their plates were empty, too.

When had they managed to polish off most of Gertrude's meal?

Her head was most definitely swimming. "Can I get you anything else, Mori? Gertrude has left a fruit tray if you'd care for something sweet."

"No, thank you."

She began clearing away the dishes, moving them to the sink, and Mori rose, helping her. She couldn't recall George ever doing such a thing, and they'd been married for ten years.

Then, when Mori rolled up his sleeves and began filling the sink with hot water, she decided she must have had *way* too much wine. "What are you doing?"

He'd discovered the narrow compartment beneath the sink. "Soap." He pulled out the bottle of liquid soap and squirted some beneath the running water. "Aids in cleaning," he explained blandly.

"Mori, you're not going to wash dishes."

He reached for a wineglass and without thought, she took hold of it, too. "You're a guest, for goodness' sake."

"And we will work faster together, than alone." He

surrounded her wrist with his free hand and gently worked the glass free of her grip to set it in the soapy bubbles. Without looking, he reached out and flipped off the water.

He did not release her wrist.

She felt parched again and swallowed, moistening her lips. "Mori—" But she didn't know what to say, so she fell silent.

"We will be concluding the merger soon." His voice was deep. Low.

"Yes." Her answer was little more than a whisper. "I…look forward to it."

"Do you?" With barely half a step, he closed what was left of the distance between them. His thumb smoothed slowly back and forth against her wrist, pressing gently against the pulse that beat there.

"Yes." This one was even more faint.

His hand slid up from her wrist to her forearm. Her elbow.

"This…isn't wise."

His hand grazed beyond her elbow to her upper arm and even higher, cupping her shoulder. "No," he agreed and lowered his head, slowly covering her lips with his.

A soft sound rose in her throat and time seemed to grind to a halt as he explored the shape of her lips, teasingly light, tempting, exploring.

Wine, she thought hazily. He tasted slightly of wine. She leaned into him, sucking in a breath when his hand slid to the small of her back.

Then there was nothing exploratory, nothing teasing. There was only heat and thick, drowning want.

She clutched his arms, feeling a need to steady herself, when there really was no need, for his arms were strong and warm and surrounding.

"Helen?"

She moaned a little, angling her head, wanting more of Mori's kiss, more of *Mori*.

"Helen? Are you here?"

Mori lifted his head, his eyebrows drawn fiercely together. "There is a woman calling for you."

"Helen?" The voice drew nearer.

Mori had barely set her away from him, putting some semblance of propriety between them, when Delia stepped into the kitchen. Andrew was right behind her.

"There you are," Delia said. "Didn't you hear me calling?"

"Sorry." Helen crossed to the woman who'd captured the heart of her youngest stepson, and kissed her cheek. "You're looking wonderful," she said truthfully, before either Delia or Andrew could question her further. "Pregnancy just seems to agree with you more every day."

Delia pressed her hand down her abdomen that seemed particularly pronounced given her petite size. "Thank you." Her blue gaze traveled beyond Helen to Mori. "Mr. Taka, it is a pleasure to see you again."

"Yes, it is." Andrew moved over to shake the man's hand. "Welcome to Chicago. My uncle told us you were having dinner here tonight." Though Andrew's voice was perfectly genial, Helen still felt his censure. "I trust my father's wife has treated you well."

"Helen is a most gracious hostess," Mori replied.

"I was just ready to set out fruit and make some coffee. You'll stay, of course? Delia, be a darling, would you, and show Mori and your groom to the library, while I finish up a few things in here."

Delia was no fool. She clearly knew she'd interrupted something. The tinge of sympathy in her eyes as she smoothly redirected the men out of the kitchen told Helen so.

The moment they were gone, Helen turned toward the sink, grabbing the edges of the counter hard enough to bruise her palms.

Get a grip on yourself, Helen Hanson.

"Helen? Are you all right?"

She straightened like a shot at the sound of her stepson's voice. "Of course, Andrew. I'm sorry that I didn't think to call you, and Evan and Meredith, as well, to join us for dinner." She quickly reached for the porcelain canister that contained ground coffee. "I don't know where my mind has been these days." She rapidly filled a filter and set the coffeemaker into action. "Did Delia's checkup go all right this afternoon?" She yanked open the refrigerator door and grabbed the fruit tray that Mori had already declined.

"Delia and the baby are both fine." Andrew eyed her closely. "You look frazzled. What's wrong?"

Nothing that some time alone with Mori wouldn't cure.

The thought had her cheeks turning hot. "You'd be frazzled, too, if you had the head of TAKA Incorporated in your home with hardly any warning," she said and thrust the tray into his hands. He had to either take it, or let the beautifully laden crystal tray fall to the floor. "Take that to the library, would you? I'll be right in with plates and napkins and such."

But Andrew, as stubborn as he had been since he was

eighteen and not at all keen on the idea of her as a step-mother, didn't budge. "Has he upset you?"

She stopped and stared. Yes, she and Andrew had made progress in the last months, just as she'd made progress with his brothers. But she hadn't taken to convincing herself that they'd made an about-face in the family love and loyalty department.

Yet Andrew—his deep brown eyes narrowed—looked truly concerned.

For her.

And the fact of it had her throat tightening. "No," she assured gently. "He hasn't upset me."

"Then why are you flushed?"

"The kitchen." She waved nonspecifically. "The oven. You know. Now, go. I'm sure Mori would like to hear about the rash of accounts you've landed this month."

"Helen." Impatience tightened the already-sharp angle of his jaw. "You *would* tell me if something were wrong."

Oh, Lord. Why did the man choose *now* to show the interest that she would have given her right arm to have in years past? She did the unthinkable and reached up to kiss his cheek. "You're a good man, Andrew. Your father would be proud of you."

A statement that only made his slightly thin lips twist. "That isn't an answer, Helen."

"It's the one you're getting," she told him, moving to a tall cupboard that housed serving trays. "Now, please. I need a few minutes of peace. I'll be right in."

"I don't like this. Something is—"

"Everything is fine." She began assembling cups and saucers on the tray she'd pulled out.

He sighed, and left with the fruit platter. She rapidly

finished preparing the coffee service, remembered in the nick of time that Mori didn't drink it, and hurriedly boiled water for tea. While she did that, she sent a hasty call to Meredith, to see if she could get her and Evan over to the house in the next few minutes.

She could, and they did, arriving only minutes after Helen carried the coffee and tea into the library. Not only had her middle stepson and his significant other come, but David and his wife, Nina, arrived with them.

Suddenly, it seemed as if the house was full of people. Someone had turned on some low music and the atmosphere had turned festive.

She busied herself refilling cups, greeting Meredith and Nina, and generally letting the Hanson men do their thing.

But across the room, Mori's gaze met hers and it made her breath grow short, all over again.

What would have happened had Delia and Andrew not interrupted them?

The look in Mori's eyes answered that.

Chapter Eight

"Helen? This is Richard. I need to know when you're going to be back in Tokyo. There is noise that Yukio Taka is planning to make a move to unseat Mori as CEO of TAKA. We need to talk."

Helen listened with disbelief to the message on her voice mail. Richard and Jenny had returned to Tokyo from their honeymoon while she was back in Chicago. She'd only spoken with them once, and had been truly glad for the conversation. She'd also wanted to call a dozen times since, but was very aware that the new relationship she was forging with Jenny was still tender. Delicate.

Now, she dialed Richard's number in Tokyo, completely disregarding the time difference. When he finally answered, his voice was full of sleep.

"'Lo?"

"Richard, it's Helen."

"It's two in the morning."

"I'm sorry. Tell Jenny I'm sorry, too. I just heard your voice mail."

"I left it yesterday."

She'd been with Mori yesterday. "I was…tied up."

"Yeah. With Mori Taka, according to Jack, who heard the news from about ten sources at Hanson. What's going on?"

She pressed her fingertips to her eyes. "That's what I'd like to know. How serious a threat is Yukio to Mori's position at TAKA?"

There was a faint delay. "Serious," Richard finally said. "He's managed to have a special board meeting called."

"On what grounds?"

"Mismanagement, conflict of interest. He may have tossed in another couple of allegations, but those are enough."

Stunned surprise struck her dumb for a long moment. "But TAKA has grown under Mori's tenure as CEO. How can that be mismanagement? And conflict of interest over *what?*"

"His personal involvement with a principal of Hanson Media Group."

She groaned, wanting to kick herself. After all the hurdles they'd run into when it came to the merger, she hadn't *once* thought of her…what—friendship?—*whatever* it was that had been growing between her and Mori as a hindrance on TAKA's part. If anything, by becoming personally involved with Mori Taka, she was more afraid of giving the man an edge *against* Hanson Media.

"There's no personal involvement," she told Richard evenly.

Mori had left that morning to return to Tokyo. He hadn't been in Chicago even twenty-four hours, and he'd been with *her* even less than that.

He'd left for his hotel when Andrew and Evan and the girls had left, since Evan and Meredith offered to drive him to his hotel.

There had been no more kisses, no more tantalizing touches. No more anything, except a call that morning to bid goodbye and to tell her that negotiations would be resumed in a week.

"What do we do about this, Richard?"

"Jack and I have an appointment in the morning. We'll draft a statement countering the allegation, but quite honestly, the TAKA board isn't looking at *us*. They're only concerned at the moment with Mori."

"But if he's unseated and his father is reinstated, Yukio will kill the merger. He's made it very plain that he doesn't approve of it. That's why Mori came to Chicago in the first place—to apologize for his father's latest tactic at the meeting Mori missed."

"Helen, you do realize that his trip there is being used as proof of Yukio's claim."

"There's nothing inappropriate going on!" But there probably would have been, had they not been interrupted. She squashed the little voice that prodded her conscience with that particular fact.

"You and he had dinner, alone, a few nights before you left Tokyo."

"His daughter was with us! Are there people *following* us?"

"Daughter present or not, Mori Taka can't make a move in Tokyo without someone taking note. Particularly when he's in the company of a beautiful blonde." Richard's voice was matter-of-fact. "At this point, TAKA stands to lose plenty if the deal is killed. They've already invested a lot of time, effort and money. Yukio may still have some pull with the board, but Mori is also on solid ground. He was second in command for fifteen years with an impeccable record, and has only seen successes in the past two since he became CEO."

"Does Mori know what's going on? He's probably in the air right now."

"He knows. Be sure of it. And he's undoubtedly taking countermeasures. Yukio Taka may have gotten the board to agree to a meeting, but that doesn't mean he has enough votes in his pocket to swing a coup against his own son. Plus, the very act of him attempting makes TAKA look bad. You know how well that's going to go over with their highly traditional board members? It won't. Don't worry, Helen. We've weathered worse and the ship hasn't yet sunk. It's not going to now, either."

"I hope you're right. I hadn't planned to come to Tokyo until the weekend. But I think I should get there now."

"Being at Mori's beck and call isn't going to help the situation."

"I'm *not* concerned about Mori." It was a blatant lie and she knew it. "Other than that—ironically—he's our best chance at finalizing the deal. But if that board thinks they're going to besmirch anything concerning Hanson—including me—I want to be there to face it."

"Well. You're the boss." Still, he sounded somewhat reluctant. "Just remember, my friend, that this isn't

Chicago. Having a woman of power challenge them has been tough as it is. We don't want to exacerbate the situation."

"Spoken like a lawyer," she said. "Look, kiss your wife for me and go back to sleep. I'll call when I get into Tokyo."

He laughed softly. "Kiss her for *you?* What about for me?"

"I have complete confidence that you've already taken care of that."

After Richard hung up, Helen sat there staring at the phone in her hand.

What would she do if the merger fell through? What would George's boys do? And Samantha and Meredith, both of whom held valuable positions with Hanson Media?

She didn't doubt for a moment any one of their abilities in finding positions elsewhere. To a one, they were talented and committed.

But they shouldn't *have* to make such a move!

She hung up the phone and picked up the gold pen she'd given George. Using it, carrying it with her, was as much talisman as reprimand. "George, what if you were wrong?"

"Wrong about what?"

She jumped, dropping the pen. It rolled across the desktop. "David. I didn't realize you were here. What can I do for you?"

He entered the room and leaned casually over the back of one of the wing chairs that sat in front of her desk. "Maybe I should be asking what I can do for you."

"I don't know what you mean."

The Silhouette Reader Service™ — Here's how it works:

Accepting your 2 free books and mystery gift places you under no obligation to buy anything. You may keep the books and gift and return the shipping statement marked "cancel." If you do not cancel, about a month later we'll send you 6 additional books and bill you just $4.24 each in the U.S., or $4.99 each in Canada, plus 25¢ shipping & handling per book and applicable taxes if any.* That's the complete price and — compared to cover prices of $4.99 each in the U.S. and $5.99 each in Canada — it's quite a bargain! You may cancel at any time, but if you choose to continue, every month we'll send you 6 more books, which you may either purchase at the discount price or return to us and cancel your subscription.

*Terms and prices subject to change without notice. Sales tax applicable in N.Y. Canadian residents will be charged applicable provincial taxes and GST. Credit or debit balances in a customer's account(s) may be offset by any other outstanding balance owed by or to the customer. Please allow 4 to 6 weeks for delivery.

If offer card is missing write to: Silhouette Reader Service, 3010 Walden Ave., P.O. Box 1867, Buffalo NY 14240-1867

NO POSTAGE
NECESSARY
IF MAILED
IN THE
UNITED STATES

BUSINESS REPLY MAIL

FIRST-CLASS MAIL   PERMIT NO. 717-003   BUFFALO, NY

POSTAGE WILL BE PAID BY ADDRESSEE

SILHOUETTE READER SERVICE
3010 WALDEN AVE
PO BOX 1867
BUFFALO NY 14240-9952

Get FREE BOOKS and a FREE GIFT when you play the...

LAS VEGAS
GAME

Just scratch off the gold box with a coin. Then check below to see the gifts you get!

YES! I have scratched off the gold box. Please send me my **2 FREE BOOKS** and **gift for which I qualify.** I understand that I am under no obligation to purchase any books as explained on the back of this card.

335 SDL EFYP   235 SDL EFXE

FIRST NAME	LAST NAME

ADDRESS

APT.#	CITY

STATE / PROV.	ZIP/POSTAL CODE

(S-SE-06/06)

| | Worth TWO FREE BOOKS plus a BONUS Mystery Gift! |
| Worth TWO FREE BOOKS! |
| TRY AGAIN! |

www.eHarlequin.com

Offer limited to one per household and not valid to current Silhouette Special Edition® subscribers. All orders subject to approval.

"Look, Helen. I know George wasn't...the best of husbands. And I didn't do a whole hell of a lot to make things easier for you while he was alive."

Her stomach tightened. "David, of all people, you were probably the easiest one to get along with."

"Sure, because we hardly had any involvement at all. I just wanted to tell you that I know it hasn't been easy for you. And I'm sorry. You've been more loyal to Hanson Media than anyone—hell, even George, considering his mismanagement and cover-up of it—and I want you to know that you're doing a good job."

She wasn't about to start bawling in the office, but she definitely felt like it. "Thank you, David. I appreciate that. But Jack would have come through if he'd been given an opportunity."

"Jack and Andrew and *particularly* Evan, after being left out of George's will, would have been happy to dump the place out of pure frustration and their feelings for the man who was their father but hardly acted like one."

"Maybe they'd have wanted to," Helen agreed softly, "but I don't think it would ever have come to pass. They'd have gone down with this ship, because it *is* Hanson."

"I'd like to think you're right. I know they would *now,* but I'm not so sure they would have eight, nine months ago. In any case, I figured it was time I said how I felt."

"You've heard from Jack, I suppose."

He nodded, and of course, he knew the ramifications if Yukio were to succeed. "Who would have thought that we'd be in a position to *want* Morito Taka in place, when he seemed to be our biggest obstacle to overcome?"

She nodded, unable to get a word out of her tight

throat. She would never forgive herself if she aided, even unknowingly, in Mori's downfall.

"So." David eyed her. "When are you leaving for Japan?"

"As soon as Sonia can book me a flight."

He nodded. "Well, have a safe flight, and I have confidence that we'll all be in Tokyo in a few weeks' time celebrating the completion."

"You'll be bringing Nina and the kids, right?"

"Wouldn't want to go anywhere without them." He lifted a hand and left her office. Only a few months had passed since he'd been a devoted bachelor. Now, he was very much a devoted family man and Helen had no worries that he'd be a distant parent like his older brother George had been.

For one thing, David adored Nina and her two children. He'd married her for the *right* reason—love.

She pushed the intercom for Sonia. "Book me the earliest flight for Tokyo."

"I'm already looking into schedules," her assistant came back. "Give me five more minutes and you'll be all set."

Satisfied, Helen grabbed the phone and her personal phone directory and made some notes to leave with Sonia. She sorted through the paperwork and files and tasks on her desk, rapidly selecting those she needed to take with her, and those that could wait until her return or be assigned to someone else.

She was just closing her jammed briefcase when Sonia entered. She handed Helen a printed itinerary. "Plane departs in three hours. I've ordered a car for you. It should be downstairs as soon as you leave, so you can run by your place and pick up some clothing. You have your passport?"

Helen nodded, skimming the itinerary. "Thanks. It's in my briefcase already. Here." She handed her assistant the notes that she'd made. "I need you to make those calls for me. And——" she patted a stack of file folders topped by a thick report "——if you can get Evan to handle this, I'd appreciate it." He was officially head of the radio division, but he'd also been pretty much acting as her replacement whenever she'd been in Japan and he'd been doing a tremendous job of it.

"This——" she tapped the middle stack "——you can take care of."

Her assistant pulled a face, but Helen knew she was perfectly willing and capable of handling the assignment. "These are the invitations that you wanted me to look over." She handed them back to Sonia. "Just send my regrets on all of them."

"Even Judge Henry's birthday celebration?" Sonia flipped through the dozen or so letters and cards.

"Send a gift…" Helen thought for a moment. "Make it a basket of chocolates. Dark, milk, white, whatever, but make sure they're individually wrapped. Small pieces that he can keep up at the bench with him. He's always telling me how he wishes he had chocolate to sweeten his disposition when he's hearing cases." She had a long-standing friendship with the elderly man dating back to the first time they'd sat on a philanthropic committee together. She was sorry to miss his party. She'd wanted to talk to him more in person about Jack's career.

"How do you remember this stuff?"

"Years of practice as the wife of George Hanson."

She slipped on her raincoat and grabbed her briefcase and purse. "Meredith's been trying to get Devlin Catering on line for the merger celebration. It might help if you give Cynthia Devlin a call. Her number's in my desk. She's a silent partner in her sister's catering firm, and she and I go way back."

"Are you sure we should start making those plans? Devlin will want a hefty deposit, given the short notice."

"Cynthia and I got our MBAs at the same time. Plus, she owes me about a million favors and that's why she won't quibble over the short notice. We want Devlin Catering because, quite simply, they are the best. And yes, I'm sure we need to plan." Her voice was determined. "Everyone in Hanson Media will be celebrating when this thing is finished. If anything else comes up, send it to Evan. Otherwise, you know where I'll be. Oh. And don't forget to feed Captain Nemo."

Sonia picked up the fishbowl. "I'll move him out there with me. He'll be in good hands. Have a safe flight."

But Helen barely heard her assistant. She was striding out of the office, her mind mostly consumed with one thing, and it wasn't the merger.

It was Mori Taka.

She reached him by phone while she was on the plane. It would be very early in Tokyo, but she suspected he'd already be at the office, and he was.

"How are you?"

He didn't pretend to misunderstand. "I have had better days."

"Mori, I'm so sorry this is happening. I feel responsible."

"Unnecessary. My father has been looking for an excuse, and he focused on the merger and you. What is the phrase your old Western movies were fond of? Rounding the wagons?"

"Circling the wagons."

"*Hai.* Circling the wagons. That is what I am doing."

"That's great, just as long as you have enough wagons," she murmured.

"I am not without some influence here," he reminded drily.

"Considering it's your own father that has taken this route, you're sounding remarkably calm."

"Should I run screaming through the hallways of TAKA?"

She almost smiled at the unlikely picture of that. "No."

"Where are you calling from? The reception is thin."

"I'm in flight."

"You are coming to Tokyo?"

She could have been flying anywhere, yet he'd automatically assumed Japan. "Yes."

"I will be glad to see you." His voice held a note that sent her pulse thudding.

"Mori—"

"You are *not* responsible for the actions of my father."

She closed her eyes, pressing the phone hard to her ear. "How do you seem to know what I'm thinking?"

"It is why I earn the large dollars."

She smiled. "You mean the big bucks."

"*Hai.* That is what I said." He was silent for a moment. "I must attend to matters here, but I will see you when you arrive."

She couldn't help the anticipation that warmed inside

her, even though she tried to steel herself against it. "That might not be the wisest course," she cautioned.

"I will see you when you arrive," he repeated.

And she didn't have the willpower to argue.

Well, wasn't she haring off to Tokyo? She might as well forget she'd ever *had* any willpower. "All right. Until then."

"Sayonara."

She disconnected the call and leaned her head back against the high seat.

"Mrs. Hanson, would you care for a cocktail?" The flight attendant stopped next to Helen's seat.

"Just coffee, please."

The beautiful girl smiled and moved to the next row in first class, repeating the spiel.

How many times would she be making this flight to Japan?

For a moment, she envied Jack and Samantha for their plan to remain in Tokyo at least for several months.

They won't need to if the merger fails.

She shushed the negative little voice. The merger could not fail.

And neither could she.

"The TAKA board is meeting tonight." Richard announced the moment Helen cleared customs. He took her carry-on suitcase from her.

"So quickly?" *Everything* seemed to be happening at breakneck speed.

"Yukio isn't wasting time. He knew Mori would still be busy dealing with his father-in-law's death. If it weren't so nasty, I'd have to give the guy points for

hitting Mori at an optimal time." He glanced her way.
"You look tired."

"Thanks. You look good. Marriage must agree with
you." She knew his first marriage certainly hadn't,
though. And while she'd definitely benefited from his
intense drive focused solely on his career for as long as
it had been, she was delighted he'd found a way to slow
down enough and not let love pass him by.

"Jenny's anxious to see you," he said, as if he'd read
her mind.

"Anxious as in worried, or anxious as in looking
forward to?"

Richard looked sympathetic. If it weren't for him, she
would never have known that Jenny Anderson was the
baby girl she'd long ago given up. But he'd recognized
the similarity and the coincidences when he'd become
involved with Jenny and had put the puzzle together.

Helen would be forever grateful to him for that.

"Looking forward to," he assured. "She has a massive
photo album from the honeymoon that she can't wait to
share."

Helen's heart squeezed. "I can't wait to see it."

Richard's pace ate up the distance as he led the way
through the very busy airport, skirting business travel-
ers and tourists with ease, and it wasn't long before
they were outside and he was heading for a waiting car.

A familiar car.

Helen's feet dragged as she recognized Mori's driver,
Akira, standing alongside the long vehicle.

Richard turned when she slowed. "What?"

"That's Mori's car."

"Handy, since he's inside."

She swallowed, suddenly nervous as a teenager. She'd been traveling for the last fifteen hours. Her hair was mussed, her suit wrinkled and if she had a lick of makeup left on her face, it would be a minor miracle.

"Well?" Richard raised his eyebrows. "Come on."

When Mori had said he would see her when she arrived, she hadn't taken him quite so literally, but painfully aware of the way Akira and Richard—and Mori, for all she knew given the darkened windows of the vehicle—were watching her, she moved forward as if she'd never hesitated at all.

"Konnichiwa," she greeted Akira when he reached out to take her heavy briefcase.

He bowed, murmuring in stilted English, "Good afternoon, Hanson-san." He quickly stowed the briefcase and the suitcase he took from Richard in the trunk then opened the rear door for them.

Helen climbed inside.

It seemed foolish, but she was grateful for Richard's presence on the facing seat when Akira closed the door and moments later the limousine began moving.

"Richard tells me the board meeting is tonight," she said, noting that Mori looked as urbane as ever in a black suit, and not at all worried about the outcome of the meeting. "You've probably got more important things to be doing than picking me up at the airport."

"I am doing exactly what I choose to be doing. Your flight was turbulent."

"How did you...never mind." Mori had his ways, and she wasn't going to wonder too hard just now about it. "It was bumpier than usual. There was a storm we had to go around, otherwise the plane would have been on time." She assumed that if Mori knew the flight conditions, he'd also known about the delay and hadn't sat, cooling his heels, in the loading zone all that time.

"Kimiko sends her greetings."

His right hand rested on the long leather seat. It was a full ten inches from her left hand, also resting on the seat.

And still, her hand felt tingly warm.

"How is she?"

"Well."

"How did you and Richard come to be together this afternoon?" She finally voiced the question that had been hovering inside her.

"Mr. Warren and I were discussing a few points of the transition."

So, they were still in an all-systems-go mode. That was good.

Knowing it didn't alleviate Helen's worry, though. It would be there, lurking under her own forcibly positive attitude until Mori's board had met.

"What points?"

"Nothing for you to be concerned with."

Helen looked across to Richard, waiting.

"Really," he assured, "it was small potatoes."

The CEO of TAKA didn't spend his time on frivolous details. And she'd foolishly thought that she and Mori were past the days when he clearly hadn't wanted to discuss even major business matters with her.

She folded her hands in her lap and looked out the window, hiding the sting she felt.

Fortunately the limo arrived quickly enough at the TAKA building. "Akira will drive you to your hotel," Mori told them. "We will speak later."

"Good luck this evening, Taka-san," Richard told him.

Mori bowed his head. "Thank you." His gaze slanted to Helen. "I am glad you are here."

She wanted badly to ask him *why,* but kept the words inside. "Good luck."

A faint smile touched his lips, and then he was gone, a tall, striking man striding into the skyscraper that bore his name.

Helen eyed Richard. "*What* little details?"

He huffed out a noisy sigh. "I knew you weren't going to let that slide."

She lifted an eyebrow. "Richard?"

"He had some questions about you, okay? That's all."

"Questions?" Her voice was not growing any warmer. "About what? And why ask you?"

"I was delivering the statement Jack and I worked on this morning and happened to mention I was picking you up from the airport. He already knew when you were arriving, and offered the car. I was pretty surprised when the guy came along, too. Just what *is* going on between you and Taka, Helen? It's clear that something beyond business has occurred."

"Well, that's terrific," Helen observed, "since it will lend credence to Yukio's ridiculous claims against Mori."

"Are they ridiculous?"

"I've said so, haven't I?"

"And I've believed you. But—"

"But *what?*"

Richard paused, very much the attorney framing his words. "The man looks at you, Helen."

She felt her face flush. "At the risk of sounding extraordinarily conceited, I'm afraid men have often *looked* at me."

Now, Richard just looked impatient. "He looks at you the way I probably look when I watch Jenny."

"That's...impossible," she said.

It was Richard's turn to raise his eyebrow. "Is it?"

from the...

Chapter Nine

That evening, Jack, Samantha and Helen went to Jenny and Richard's apartment for dinner.

Despite the cheerful face everyone put on, and the true enjoyment Helen felt when Jenny pulled out the photograph albums of the honeymoon, it felt more like a wake than a family get-together.

They were *all* waiting on word from the board meeting.

Jenny eventually turned on the television and they watched the news channel to see if there would be mention of a TAKA coup. She also made a few calls to her associates.

No one seemed to know anything.

By eleven o'clock that night, Helen was simply dragging.

She had slept a few hours on the flight, but other than

that, she hadn't put her head on a bed pillow in more than twenty-four hours.

"Much as I'd like to stick it out with you youngsters, I've got to get some sleep."

Richard snorted. He and Jack were both only a handful of years younger than she. "Nice try, Helen. You're still not gonna pass for a gray-haired granny, even when we make you one."

Her gaze flew to Jenny's, who blushed and shrugged. "Not yet," she said, "but there have been some negotiations."

The first real smile Helen had felt since the previous morning hit her face. "I think that sounds great," she told Jenny, and couldn't keep herself from hugging her.

Her eyes stung when Jenny hugged her in return.

Then they were gathering jackets and purses and heading out into the cool evening to hail a taxi.

Count your blessings where they are, Helen reminded herself. Whatever happens with the merger, she'd found Jenny and the boys had found their loves.

Wasn't *that* more important than anything else?

Alone in her hotel room, she took a shower, realized she'd forgotten to pack any nightclothes and wrapped herself in the plush white bathrobe provided by the hotel.

Despite her exhaustion, though, she couldn't relax enough to climb into bed.

She stepped between the heavy drawn curtains and the window and looked out at the city lights.

Was the board meeting still in progress?

She imagined that she could see the shape of the TAKA building, but knew it was unlikely. Her window faced east and the TAKA building was west.

Sighing, she rested her forehead against the window-pane. It felt chilly to the touch.

They were supposed to sign the final paperwork any day now. A gala celebration would shortly follow for the employees in both Japan and Chicago, the media and every mucky-muck in both countries.

Would that still come to pass?

Her head hurt from thinking about it.

Tugging the lapels closer around her, she slipped from between the heavy drapes and headed to her bed, but a soft knock on her door stopped her.

Jack or Samantha, she thought, immediately crossing the room and throwing open the door. "Have you heard—"

She stared at Mori, her words drying up.

He looked like hell. His face was tired, his eyes bloodshot.

His tie was loose, his jacket bunched in his fist.

Without thinking, she stepped back, silently inviting him inside.

He entered, pulling his tie even looser.

She closed the door, leaning back against it, and watched him cross the room. He tossed aside his jacket and went immediately to the bar and opened the small refrigerator that was stocked with every known assortment of alcohol.

She'd never bothered touching it.

But given Mori's countenance, she strongly considered the need for a stiff shot of something.

He pulled out a bottle she didn't recognize the name on, and dumped the contents in one of the squat crystal glasses that sat atop the bar.

When he'd finished, he turned, drink in hand, and looked at her.

Her hands balled in the deep pockets of her robe. "Are you all right?"

"My father saw the wisdom of retracting his request." He drank half the contents of his glass in one long drink, then moved to the couch and sat on it.

His head bowed and he stared at the drink held loosely in his hands.

She went over and sat beside him. "That ought to sound like good news," she said softly. "But you look like a man who has lost the war, rather than winning it."

"There is no winning when my father has made known to everyone that he has no faith in me."

She started to put her hand on the back of his neck and realizing it, curled her fingers, drawing back before touching him. "You say he took back his request of the board, though."

"*Hai.*"

"Didn't they wonder why?"

"*Hai.*" His voice turned very dry. "My father claimed illness prompted his behavior. He, who has never been *ill* in his life."

"So there was no board meeting at all?"

"There was a meeting, during which I received many votes of confidence."

"Well, that's good, right? Your position is still secure?"

"You need not worry. The board will not overturn the decision to acquire Hanson Media Group."

She stiffened. Yes, she'd been rightfully concerned about the merger, but the moment she'd seen Mori

looking so *un*-Mori, she'd only had thoughts of him.
"Merger," she reminded him evenly.

His dark gaze turned to her. *"Sumimasen,"* he said.
"Pardon me. *Merger.*" He quaffed the rest of his drink
and leaned forward, setting the glass with inordinate
care on the gilt-edged coffee table. "Your father is still
alive, is he not?"

"Yes," she said warily. "Why?"

"You do not have a good relationship?"

"No, we do not." She pushed to her feet, tightening
the belt of her robe. "And I suspect that you, with your
wealth of ways, know why that is."

"He forced you to give up your baby when you were
little more than a baby yourself."

"I was sixteen. At the time I didn't feel much like a
baby."

"Kimiko is twelve."

"At that age, four years' difference might as well be
a lifetime." She truly didn't know where this was going,
but she knew she wasn't comfortable with it.

She hadn't spoken with her father since the day he'd
held her arms when she'd tried running after the adop-
tion representative carrying away her child. And though
she'd kept in touch with her brother while their mother
was alive, the contact had been inevitably awkward.
She'd wanted to make her mother's life easier—what
good was the wealth Helen had surprisingly married
into, if she couldn't bring more comfort to the people
she'd loved?

They seemed to think she was only trying to lord it
over them. Her brother had been barely willing to pass
on the financial assistance she'd sent for her mother to

have in the guise of a gift from him. If it were anything other, she knew her father would have made sure their mother would not accept it. Now, in the years since Helen's mother had passed away, she'd spoken to Walt only twice. He'd made it clear he had no use for her, just like their father.

"My father left me no choice about the baby," she said. "But bringing a child into *that* family wasn't something I wanted to do. It was bad enough for my brother and me. I wasn't going to subject any child of mine to an atmosphere like that."

"Like what?"

She smoothed back her hair only to catch her fingertips in the thong holding it in a ponytail. She pulled it loose and stuck it in her pocket. Her hair slid over her shoulder. "Controlling. Unloved. My father and mother *had* to get married when she became pregnant with my older brother, Walt. The day I told my parents that I was pregnant, my dad looked at Mom and told her that it was all *her* fault. I was just like her, trying to trap another innocent guy."

"Unwed pregnancies have been occurring through the ages, even in my country."

"And causing plenty of scandal," she reminded pointedly.

His gaze didn't waver from hers and she knew that he still didn't feel badly for halting the negotiations when the truth about Jenny came out.

"Did your husband know about the child?"

First her father, now George. "Why does it matter to you, Mori? It's all water under the bridge." Dark, churning water.

"Did he?"

She couldn't fathom what possessed her to answer. "No, he didn't."

"Why did you not tell him?"

"This has nothing to do with tonight's board meeting."

He pushed to his feet and headed toward her. Slowly. Deliberately. "It has to do with *you.*"

"Obviously, considering your questions are *about* me. Why do you care?"

"I do not know!" His voice rose slightly and he grimaced. "Why do I jeopardize everything I have worked for my entire life to visit you here, at this hotel, when anyone could have seen me enter the doors and speculate which room I visit? I could have a dozen lovers and not surprise a soul, but I visit with Helen Hanson, head of Hanson Media, and I am looked at with suspicion by men who have worked with me for decades."

She winced. "I'm sorry they all find me so offensive."

"You are not offensive, Helen, you are a *gaijin* businesswoman, playing on *their* field, and they do not like it when they suspect I have joined your team. TAKA is not accustomed to negotiations like this. You are surely aware of it. TAKA takes *over* companies. Yet *you* have kept us at the table while still managing to prevent that from happening. It is…remarkable."

At any other time, she would have been deeply pleased by the comments—not exactly praising given his position, but definitely giving her full measure. "This whole thing is insane. You and I are *not* involved, except across the bargaining table."

He touched her cheek. "Are we not?"

She swallowed. "This is what's getting us into trouble in the first place."

"Yet here I am, even though most people would consider me to be the most practical and traditional of men."

"Well, maybe just like many men, you only want to get me in the sack. *Bed,*" she clarified at his blank look.

"Do you *sack* with many men?"

"I don't think that's any of your business."

His thumb slid beneath her chin, then along her jaw until he held her face captive.

Her heart bounced around unevenly. She lifted her chin, just to prove that she could move away if she chose.

His hand didn't move.

"No," she finally said huskily. "I don't *sack,* as you say, with men. I was married for ten years. And before that, way before that, was Jenny's father. So do not even try to lecture me."

Mori's eyelids drooped a fraction more until only a thin gleam of brown showed between his thick lashes. "Did he lecture you a lot?"

"Who?" Now was not the time to get confused by the man's intense physical appeal. "My father? He was an unending lecture."

"Your late husband."

"The only thing George lectured me about was my waistline, the length of my hair and why he wanted me to stay out of Hanson Media."

"He was a fool not to recognize he held a pearl in his hands."

"Don't stand there and pretend that you welcomed me in the conference room with open arms, Mori. You detested me."

"You disturbed me," he corrected softly, closing the distance between them by half. "But it is true that you are not the typical person with whom I deal."

"You have business dealings in other countries than Japan," Helen reminded. "You don't have female associates in London?"

"In London, yes. But they do not come to my country and challenge me under my own roof."

"Just because I want what's reasonable and fair for Hanson Media doesn't mean I'm challenging you."

A faint smile hovered around his lips. "You are challenging me even now."

"I—" she pressed her lips together for a moment. When she thought she could speak without debating yet another point, thereby proving the man correct, she tried again. "What exactly do you want, Mori?"

"In general, in life, or in this moment?"

"This moment."

"I want you."

Her mouth dried. Well, she'd asked, hadn't she?

"Despite all the reasons why I should not, why it would be better that I did not, I still want you. And I keep choosing to see you because of it."

Her lashes lowered. Her hands twisted in the sash of her robe. "You said you came to Chicago to apologize for your father and Shiguro."

"And I spoke the truth. I also came because I wanted—needed—to see you. Apologies *can* be offered over the telephone." He closed his hands over her fidgeting ones. "Do you not wish to see me, also?"

"Mori—"

"Do you?"

"Yes." The word was more a breath.

"One day—" he lowered his head close to hers, whispering softly against her ear "—it will be just you and me. A woman and a man. No contracts, no lawyers. Only us. Only this." His lips touched her jaw. His hands lifted hers until they were caught between their torsos.

Her knees felt weak. She spread her fingers and they tangled in the trailing ends of his magenta tie. She slowly pulled the knot loose. "And what about *this* day?" Her voice was faint.

"This day I am TAKA and you are Hanson Media."

It was frightening how badly she wanted him to stay. How hard it was to focus on the reasons why he should not.

The only times in her life when she'd put reason and common sense behind a locked door, she'd ended up paying a high price. The first, she'd been just sixteen when she fell in love with a jock named Drew Sheffield. He hadn't stood beside her when she'd needed him— he'd run hightail to his parents, who'd quickly moved him out of town lest he have his aspirations tainted by poor little Helen Needham.

The second time, she'd married George Hanson, a man twenty-seven years her senior who'd swept her off her feet so quickly she hadn't even *tried* to find her common sense.

Drew had just been a boy too young to face the consequences of their actions and George had used her love for him for his own purposes, only acknowledging her business acumen when he'd had no other recourse.

What would throwing common sense to the wind do now?

Could she even take a chance at finding out?

"You have had a long day," Mori murmured, brushing his lips over hers, successfully eroding another layer of sensibility. "You need sleep. Tomorrow we resume the negotiations. I have had messages sent to all the parties involved. We have much work to do to become back on schedule."

She was painfully aware of all the work they had yet to accomplish—points on which they had yet to agree. "I thought we would be waiting until next week because of your father-in-law's passing."

"Do *you* wish to delay still?"

She shook her head. The closer they got to the end, the worse the pressure got. She wanted the deal signed and delivered.

Only then would she feel like the last ten years of her life had actually *meant* something.

"No, I don't want any more delays." Because she didn't think she'd rest again if she didn't, she leaned up and pressed her mouth against his.

His hand slid through her hair, cupping the back of her head, fingers flexing against her scalp.

She could have purred, and was gratified that when they pulled apart, his breath was as short as hers.

"You have to go," she told him huskily.

"I know."

Her head fell forward, resting against his chest. "I don't want you to." The admission felt raw.

His arms closed around her back and he held her so close that she suddenly felt like crying.

Which only served to remind her of the night of Jenny's wedding when he'd caught her in tears.

"I do not want to leave you, either," he said.

"It's a mistake. The last two days are proof of that."

"What do you worry about more, Helen?" Mori's chest rumbled beneath her cheek as he spoke. "Undoing the merger, or being with a man other than your husband?"

She didn't want to think about George anymore. "My husband and I hadn't shared a bed in several years."

"Because of his age?"

"He might have been sixty-eight, but he was a *young* sixty-eight."

He tilted her head back until her face was exposed. "He had other women?"

How many times had she wondered that, herself? "I don't think so. George's only mistress was Hanson Media."

"Then why?"

She closed her eyes. "I'm not asking you questions about the relations you had with your wife."

"We lived together as man and wife only long enough to conceive Kimiko."

"At least you were lucky enough to *conceive* a child."

He was silent for a moment and she made the mistake of opening her eyes. He was watching her with that disturbing intensity—seeming to see into her very soul.

"You wished to have another child," he surmised.

Her throat was tightening up again. She didn't want to feel all that emotion. If she had to feel anything, she wanted it to be the drugging pleasure he caused—even if that *were* the height of folly given the circumstances.

"Helen?"

"Yes. For the first six years we were married, we tried

everything, every conceivable treatment, even nontraditional methods. There was nothing physically wrong with George, nothing physically wrong with me."

"Yet—"

"No child." She pulled out of his arms, feeling too naked and vulnerable to stay so close to him. "Maybe that was my karma. I'd given away one child, so I wasn't to be allowed another."

"I am not certain that is an accurate definition of karma," he said softly, and the simple gentleness in his voice had her eyes flooding.

"How about God's punishment, then?"

His head tilted slightly. "It was just not meant to be. My wife killed herself because of her lack of interest in the life she had and for the child she'd borne."

Helen was shocked out of the painful memories that sucked at her. "I had no idea."

"Why would you?"

Because she'd investigated very thoroughly every aspect of TAKA and its principals before she'd put her plan for Hanson Media into action. "What happened?"

"Sumiko was not a strong woman like you are." He tapped his finger against his head. "Here."

Helen wrapped her arms around herself. She didn't feel particularly strong. She felt shaky and hopelessly without common sense.

"When Kimiko was still an infant, her mother began spending more time away from her. Traveling. Going out at night with friends. I was too immersed in TAKA to see what was happening at first. When I realized she was addicted to alcohol and drugs, I made sure she had treatment, and she became better for a while. But it did not last. Eventually, her body could not sustain the abuse she heaped on it."

"Kimiko was only a baby."

"Yes."

She shook her head. "I'm so sorry, Mori. What an awful thing to have happen to all three of you."

"If I were to use your example of karma, I would believe that I will never be able to be a husband again, because I had already failed to keep safe the wife I did have."

She pressed her lips together for a moment. "You wish to marry again some day?"

"I do not wish to be alone for the rest of my life," he answered.

Which wasn't really an answer at all.

"I was responsible for my wife, but I have realized that I could not force her to change her life. She had to want change from within badly enough to put up a fight and take the help she was offered from all sides. But she did not."

"Did you love her?" She realized she was holding her breath and made herself let it out slowly when he took his time answering.

"I loved her for the child she gave me."

"Then at least there was that."

"You still grieve for the man that did not share your bed."

"I grieve for the marriage I thought I'd had." The truth burned. "I loved my husband, and I thought he loved me. Turns out I was wrong, and I'm afraid I'm finding that reality more difficult than accepting his death."

"Why do you believe he did not love you?"

She didn't know what possessed her to reveal such

matters. Was it because he'd shared the facts about his wife?

Were the details of his past any less painful than hers?

She went into the bedroom and picked up the jewelry case from the dresser and started to carry it back out, but he stepped into the bedroom after her.

Her nerves tightened even more.

"I *know*, because he told me." She set down the case and pulled out George's letter to her. It was the devil inside her that handed the sheet of stationery to him. "Everything I'd believed about myself, about my marriage, turned out to be nothing more than wishful thinking."

Mori glanced down the letter only long enough to grasp the gist. He was not overly shocked by the contents. George Hanson had only done what Mori's father believed he had done in arranging Mori's marriage to Sumiko when they were nothing but infants.

He'd made an advantageous match.

The difference was, Sumiko had been perfectly aware of the point of the union. Helen, clearly, had not.

He wondered which was worse.

Refolding the letter, he lifted the lid of the wooden box himself to place it inside.

As he did so, he noticed a crisp dried leaf lying alongside a thin silver bracelet.

The leaf from their walk in the park?

A muscle was working in Helen's fine jaw, proof of her tension. He placed the letter inside the box and closed the lid, hiding the leaf and all the rest once more.

"It is difficult to have one's life manipulated," he told her. "There are things we can control, and things we cannot. I could not control Sumiko, and you could not control George. That does not mean you were wrong to love him."

Her long, lovely throat worked in a swallow.

"Nor does it mean you were foolish."

She turned her head slightly, but not quickly enough for him to miss the sheen of tears in those jade eyes. "I wasted ten years trying to be the woman he wanted, and it turns out he didn't care, anyway. Believe me, Mori. That feels *extremely* foolish."

"And now, you are still trying to be the woman he wanted, by ensuring Hanson Media Group does not fold?"

Her posture straightened. She leveled him a long look, shaking her hair back a little until it rippled over her shoulders like cool moonlight. "I'm doing *that* to prove to myself that I'm more than just George Hanson's trophy wife, and to make sure that my stepsons don't lose their entire heritage because of their father's poor judgment. Whether they like it or not, they *are* my family and I want them to have everything they deserve."

"They do not know of this." He tapped the top of the jewelry box.

She looked horrified. "Of course not. I don't want their pity. As far as that goes, I shouldn't have told *you*."

As far as Mori was concerned, he was not entirely convinced her stepsons merited her championship. But he recognized one thing.

Helen Hanson was more deeply honorable than he would ever have believed just a short while ago. She might not describe her actions as that, but the result was the same.

She was caring for her family in whatever manner she could.

And the reasons why he should leave, immediately, were becoming harder to obey when the reasons why he should stay were gaining a strength that he could not deny. That he did not *want* to deny.

Chapter Ten

"It has been a day of revelation," Mori murmured, taking a step toward her and feeling a jolt of satisfaction when she made a nervous movement as a result.

Helen's hand tightened over the lapels of her robe, holding them together. But her green eyes were *not* afraid.

He realized he had never seen her truly afraid of anything and it, too, was a heady realization.

He closed his hands over her shoulders. She was slender, but he did not have a sense that she was fragile. "You need to sleep," he reminded.

Her chin lifted a little. "So do you."

When had he thought her voice was not musical? Her low words stroked over his nerves with a mellow tone.

He smoothed his hand down her hair. "You do not often wear your hair down."

Her eyes nearly closed, and her head pressed against his palm, like a cat unconsciously seeking petting.

"It's easier pulled back."

He slowly threaded his fingers through the strands. It was thick. Smooth and silky and infinitely pale against his hand. "I have dreamed of you."

Her lips parted and he saw another swallow work down her throat. "You...have?"

"That surprises you? It should not. You have been consuming my thoughts much longer than I wish to admit."

Her lips curved. "How long?"

"Always wanting to clarify the details."

"That would be me," she agreed. Her fingers slid inside his shirt collar. Rested against his pulse that beat heavily, only to move again, finding a button and toying with it.

"I have wanted you from the beginning," he admitted.

She made a soft sound. Of disagreement?

"I believed I could want and not touch, however, until the night Kimiko made her hair pink. At dinner."

"We did nothing but have dinner that evening."

"You asked when, not why."

She lifted her lashes, slanting a look up at him. "How is it that you can get me to want to laugh, after a day like this has been?"

"Laughing is good," he murmured, "but it is not my specific goal at the moment."

"And you are a goal-oriented man."

"*Hai.*"

She continued toying with his button. He wondered how long she intended to torment him in such a manner.

"If I might ask, what *is* your specific goal?"

He flattened his hand over her tantalizing fingertips, stilling them against his chest. "You."

Her eyes darkened. "We have established that isn't a wise decision."

He traced the lapel of her robe from her neck, down the slope of her breast to the belt that was, even now, falling loose. "I am thinking right now that wisdom is rated too highly."

She moistened her lips. Swallowed. "Is that so?"

He slowly pulled the loop of her belt free. The thick white terry cloth began to part.

She caught his wrists in her hands. "Mori."

She was shaking. He frowned. "You do not wish this."

"No!" She shook her head, her cheeks turning pink. "I—I do. Really. It's just—I haven't—" She raked her fingers through her hair, holding it back from her face. "I'm sorry. I'm a grown woman, I should be better at this. But I told you. George and I didn't...hadn't... it...it's just been a while," she finished in a rush. "A really long while."

He slid his hands along her jaw, cupping her face. She was blushing and he wanted her more than ever. "Are you in need of a refresher course?"

She stared at him for a moment, seemingly speechless. Then a soft smile touched her lips. "Perhaps I am. *Sensei* is the word for teacher?"

"It has a wider reference, but yes."

"Sensei," she repeated. Her fingers returned to his shirt collar, sliding over it, then under it and his skin heated wherever her gliding grazed. "So...refresh me."

He tilted her chin up, lowering his head toward hers.

"First, there is the touch." He slipped his fingers beneath the thick skein of pale hair and touched the nape of her neck. Drew his fingertip down the line of her spinal cord. She trembled against him, her own fingers faltering unsteadily.

"Mori." His name sounded like a soft ache in her husky voice. "The...light?"

He had no desire to turn off the single lamp burning near the bed. "Second is the kiss," he continued and kissed the corner of her eye.

Her lashes fluttered like butterfly wings against his lips. "But—"

"Why do you wish to hide in the dark, Helen?" He kissed the high curve of her cheekbone.

"I don't hide," she defended, arching against him when his hand slid over the robe as he explored the long length of her back.

"You wish the darkness," he murmured against her ear before he caught her unadorned earlobe between his lips.

Her head twisted against his shoulder, her fingers knotting in his shirt. "I wish I were a decade or two younger," she muttered. *"Oh."* She moaned softly when he pressed his mouth against the side of her neck.

He pulled at the sleeve of her robe and it slid unimpeded, over her shoulder, falling down to her bent elbow. He lifted his head to study his work. If she knew the way he had to work to form thoughts when he would rather just stare at the perfection before him, she would never make such a comment.

He drew her head up from where it was pressed against his shoulder. He caught a flash of vulnerability in her eyes before her lashes swept down, hiding it. "I have no desire to be with a girl twenty years younger than me. I wish a partner who matches me. I wish for you."

She caught her lip between her teeth. He tsked and rubbed his thumb over the tiny spot and felt her indrawn breath when she dragged in a breath.

"What is the third thing to remember?"

"The heart."

She drew one of her palms down the center of his chest to rest over his heart. "You are a romantic," she whispered. "Who would have thought it?"

"I am a man and I want a woman," he corrected huskily. He mimicked her actions, drawing his hand down the center of her chest until he felt her heartbeat racing against his palm. The robe fell off her other shoulder, fully baring her body to him.

She wasn't an ivory candle, slender and tall and unlit.

She was golden and warm and wherever, whenever he touched, she seemed to glow.

And he ached.

"I think it's coming back to me," she said huskily, and covered his hand with hers, sliding her fingers between his for a moment, then retreating to his wrist for a moment, only to return to his fingers. Her heart raced beneath their joined hands and she shifted slightly, her gaze on his face as she drew his hand over the swell of her breast. Her lips parted, her gaze flickering.

His hand tightened on her breast, circled the rigid peak that rose greedily to his touch, then his taste.

Her head fell forward again, her cool hair sliding over them both. "Take me to bed, Mori," she whispered.

He kicked aside her robe and pulled her tightly against him.

She inhaled sharply. "You know I like things to be fair." Her hands worked between them to tear at his shirt buttons.

He caught her lips with his, helping her and in moments, his clothes were a thing of the past.

Her arms clung around his shoulders as he backed her to the bed, following her down. Her hair streamed around them and her eyes glowed in the soft light.

"Let me see if I remember, now. Touch." She dragged her fingertips down the length of his spine and a faint smile touched her lips when he let out a low breath.

"Hai."

Her knee slowly slid along his thigh. She pressed her mouth against his chest, tasting him. "Kiss."

"Hai." He caught her head in his hands and kissed her deeply.

The green of her eyes turned glassy when he lifted his head and staring into them, he slid against her. She made a soft sound, her arms tightening against him. Her legs tangled with his. "Please. My heart can't take teasing."

"No teasing," he promised, and slowly, inexorably pressed into her.

She moaned his name and he exhaled roughly, curving over her. But she lifted herself against him, removing any protective distance he would have created between him and her slender body, which was already quaking against him.

She was welcoming and warm, and female to male, and if he'd held any notion of control, it was suddenly lost.

His hands found her hips and he sank deeply.

She cried out and held him even closer, twining herself around him. "Yes," she gasped. "Yes."

Then the lapping waves of her shuddering pleasure became a tidal wave that dragged him under.

And he was drowning with her, for nothing in life had ever prepared him for a woman like Helen.

Helen overslept the next morning.

It wasn't until she heard the heavy pounding on her hotel room door that she finally opened her eyes and stared at the empty pillow next to hers on the bed.

The tumbled covers helped assure her that she hadn't merely dreamed of Mori.

Not this time.

He hadn't stayed the rest of the night, which wasn't much of a night, given the dawn light that had been slipping around the window drapes when he left.

She'd wanted him to stay. But it was simply too fool-hardy for him to do so.

Knowing it didn't make her miss him any less, however.

Another pounding rattled the door from the living area. She heard the muffled sound of her name being called.

Feeling lazy and not entirely rested, she glanced at the clock on the bedside table.

The time finally registered.

"Oh, *hell.*" She jumped out of the bed, grabbing up the robe that was lying on the floor. She was just tying the sash when she reached the door.

A glance through the peephole revealed Jack's face, his expression as thunderous as his pounding.

She opened the door, already turning away before he

could step inside. "Give me ten minutes, and I'll be ready to go."

"Jesus, Helen." He entered the suite behind her, slamming the door. "I thought something was wrong!"

First Andrew's concern and now Jack's. Oh, they were such surprising men.

"I'm fine," she assured. "I just overslept." She raced into the bedroom, closing the door behind her. The shower water wasn't even warm before she was jumping back out of it and toweling off. She flipped on the blow dryer, directing it through her hair long enough that she could pin it into a chignon without looking like a wet cat, and forced herself to slow down enough to apply some makeup without smearing mascara or lipstick over her face. She didn't seem to need much color, anyway. Her lips were pinker than usual. Fuller than usual, too.

Thinking about the reason for that slowed her movements when she had no time to spare, so she just would not think about it.

But every movement she made as she stepped into an ivory-colored suit made a mockery of that particular vow.

There wasn't a part of her that didn't bear the memory of Mori's touch.

She shoved her feet into her shoes and went back out to join Jack. "I'm sorry. I just need my briefcase."

He picked it up off the table where she'd left it and handed it to her. "I thought you always left a wake-up call."

"I do." She took the case from him and headed for the door. The last thing she wanted was for Jack to begin speculating. "I didn't sleep much last night." That was true enough. "I guess I slept through the call this morning."

"And Samantha's when I couldn't get you to answer the door?"

"Evidently. Oh. My room key." She glanced around. The small credit-card-size piece of plastic was on the coffee table.

Next to Mori's glass from the night before.

Worse, it was within a foot of Mori's jacket, laying on the end of the couch. Jack *had* to have noticed it.

She snatched up the key and turned back to the door. Her feet dragged to a halt, though, at Jack's low voice.

"Whose jacket is that?"

"Mine," she lied blatantly, and grabbed his arm, hustling him out the door, which she slammed behind her.

"Right. Looks like it'd *fit* you, too, Helen, if you grew about half a foot and gained about sixty pounds." He caught her arm, stopping her in her tracks. "Who was here?"

She gave him a long look. The elevator door slid open beside them. "Actually, Jack, that isn't your business."

"Dammit, Helen, Samantha and I were *concerned*."

"And I appreciate it," she said sincerely. "But there is nothing to be concerned about. Now let's get to this meeting. Obviously, you got the message from TAKA."

"A courier brought by a schedule last night after we got back from Jenny and Richard's."

Mori hadn't mentioned a schedule. She punched the button for the lobby floor and the elevator began its dizzying descent.

"It was Mori Taka, wasn't it?"

She swallowed. "He came to tell me what happened at the board meeting."

"And *left* his jacket."

"Is that so unlikely?"

"Why did he take it off in the first place?"

"For pity's sake, Jack. This isn't the Inquisition. The man came to speak with me. I offered him a drink. Do you think it was *easy* for him to face that meeting yesterday? His own father was trying to undermine him." She shot him a look. "You of all people should have some sympathy over that."

His expression only tightened. "You never change, do you, Helen? One wealthy husband is out of the way, so you're looking for another? I really thought I might have been wrong about you before, but I wasn't, was I? I'll give you credit, though. At least this one isn't old enough to be your damned father, *and* he could buy and sell Hanson Media several times over. Nice work."

He might as well have slapped her.

She stared hard at the number display but his anger was a physical thing sucking all the oxygen out of the small space. She actually felt dizzy.

"I haven't given up everything I've worked for to see the deal go down the tubes because you and Mori can't keep your hands off each other. The man's not going to be interested in you forever, you know. You're an American, for God's sake, and he's about as Japanese as they come."

The elevator doors opened and Jack stepped off.

She followed him slowly, vaguely surprised that he'd bothered to keep the taxi waiting for her. Without a word, she climbed in beside him.

The drive to the TAKA building had never seemed to take so long.

Wasn't it the height of irony that in finding one night—not even an entire *night*, for that matter—of happiness with a man, she would end up losing what little progress she'd made with the family that had never wanted her, anyway?

She could feel Jack's sidelong look and deliberately pulled out her leather portfolio and flipped it open to her notes.

She didn't read a single word of them.

The meeting ran through lunch, which was brought in on several rolling carts and distributed around the conference table.

It was Italian food, and the sight of the lasagna, garlic bread and green salad made Helen want to laugh.

Hysterically.

Mori had not said one word personally to her since the moment he'd entered the room and taken his place at the head of the table.

He'd barely looked at her, for that matter.

Jack, however, seemed to be looking from Mori to her and back again. She didn't need a degree in rocket science to interpret the "I told you so" look in Jack's eyes when he happened to catch her gaze.

She jabbed her fork into a lettuce leaf and ignored *all* of the men surrounding her.

The lunch break was mercifully brief, and the meeting resumed.

About a hundred years later, it concluded.

Helen tucked her pen in her portfolio and closed it, pushing back from the table.

Mori cast her an inscrutable look.

Well, she'd known that their relationship would remain private, hadn't she?

It wasn't as if he could go around crowing that he'd slept with Helen Hanson, after all. Mori's father might have recanted his accusation, but that didn't mean that he couldn't put it forward yet again. Or that someone else within TAKA couldn't do it for him.

Still, the complete lack of acknowledgment in Mori's demeanor toward her *hurt*. He was even cooler to her than he had been at the very beginning.

As if such a thing were possible.

She squared her shoulders, though, and looked around the occupants of the room as they began pushing back from the table. "Have a good evening, gentlemen. I look forward to tomorrow."

She angled toward Mori, bowed and then strode out of the room, uncaring of the stunned silence that her abrupt departure caused.

Chapter Eleven

"Here." A glass of red wine appeared in Helen's line of sight. She followed the glass to the feminine hand that held it to the woman it belonged to. "You look like you need it," Samantha continued.

Helen slowly took the glass. It was nearly midnight and she was sitting at a small round table next to a window in the hotel's top floor cocktail lounge. She'd never been up there before, and it had seemed an admirable choice when she hadn't wanted to remain alone in her hotel room all evening.

Instead, she'd sat alone at this table, staring out at the lights and wondering what had become of her life. "Thanks." She silently toasted the other woman with the glass before taking a sip. She had half a dozen empty glasses on the table. None of them had contained a drop of alcohol. "Who would have thought, back when I was once your babysitter, that we'd be on the other side of the world like this?"

"I'll take that as an invitation," Samantha said, as she slid into the chair opposite Helen.

"Sorry." Helen shook herself. "Of course, join me."

"As long as I don't have Jack with me?" Samantha's gaze was sympathetic. "He told me you two had words this morning before the meeting."

"That's one way of putting it."

"He didn't mean it, Helen."

She lifted her eyebrows. "I never realized just *how* optimistic you were, Samantha." She tilted her glass again in the other woman's direction. "Here's to the hope that that trait always serves you well."

"He's stressed out over the merger. And he's somewhat unnerved over the fact that he's realizing you aren't the woman he's always made you out to be."

"Samantha, I love you. I'm glad you and Jack are together and making each other happy. But I do not want to talk about this."

"Well, maybe you get to call the shots a little too often, Helen," Samantha countered gently. "Come on. We're a family. Families say stuff all the time that they don't really mean."

Helen drank the wine down in only a few gulps. Family? She wanted badly to think so, but reality had a way of eroding such hopes. "Does Jack know you're up here?" She could tell by Samantha's expression that he did not. "Go back to your husband, sweetheart, and don't worry about me. I'm fine."

Samantha let out a long breath. She rose and came

around to Helen's side, dropping a kiss on her head. "You're not fine and *families* are allowed to worry, whether *you* like it or not."

"She is right."

Helen nearly toppled the wineglass at Mori's voice. She looked past Samantha at him. "Where did you come from?"

"Nesutotaka," he said calmly.

Her lips tightened. "Very funny."

"Join Jack and me for breakfast before tomorrow's session," Samantha whispered for Helen's ears, then she turned to Mori and bowed. "Good evening, Mr. Taka. If you'll excuse me?"

He returned the greeting. "Of course, Mrs. Hanson."

Samantha shot Helen another look as she hurried out of the bar.

Mori took the seat that Samantha had occupied so briefly. "I have been calling your room."

She focused her gaze somewhere around his temple. Anything to avoid looking in those black-brown eyes of his. "Really? Why?"

"To speak with you."

"I think our speaking together should be kept in the conference room, don't you?"

He reached across the table and caught her chin, moving it an inch until her gaze met his. "What has upset you? You were not yourself at our meeting today, either."

The glass of wine had been a mistake, just as it always was. "I guess I find it harder than I thought it would be to face the man I spent hours making love with across a negotiating table."

"Do you regret it?"

Her throat tightened. "The way you must?"

"I did not say that *I* did."

She leaned toward him, keeping her voice carefully low. "Well, what *do* you feel, Mori? Because I have realized that I do not have the first clue when it comes to reading you."

"Do you wish that I would sweep you into my arms like some foolish American movie regardless of the setting? It was a *meeting,* Helen."

"No, I don't wish you to act like some besotted idiot in a stupid movie! I expect…I expect…oh, damn!" She pushed back from the table. "I don't know what I expect, that's how badly you've got me twisted up. Look, I am a big girl. Last night was…a diversion for both of us. A one-time deal where we both got what we wanted out of it."

He stood also, his expression hardening. "That is what you believe?"

"What else can I believe, Mori? You looked right through me today." She hated the fact that her voice caught. She wasn't a teenager begging her boyfriend not to desert her when he left her pregnant. She was a forty-one-year-old adult who, for years and years, had been playing the cards her life had dealt.

So why did she feel as if she hadn't learned one thing in all that time? And why did everything seem to hurt more now?

"It's late. I'm going to bed. I'll see you tomorrow at TAKA." She turned away.

He caught her arm, preventing her from getting more than two inches.

She looked up at his face and was abruptly reminded

of the night he'd held the Samurai sword in his suite at the Anderson hotel.

Her mouth dried.

"I could not *look* at you without giving away my feelings," he said grimly. "Is that what you wish to hear, Helen? Do you *want* my brother and my associates to know from my expression or my actions that I am consorting with you?"

"Consorting with the enemy, you mean? We're not enemies, Mori. You and I both want the same thing—for Hanson Media to be part of TAKA Corporation. Why do you think I made sure you even *heard* of Hanson Media?"

The challenge seemed to linger in the air long after it should have.

"You sent a prospectus."

"A good six weeks after I knew you'd already been investigating the advantages of an acquisition," she said tiredly. "I made sure that Hanson Media was on the list of companies you routinely review for acquisition."

"How?"

"I was the wife of George Hanson. I worked with more committees for more social functions or philanthropic events than you can possibly imagine. I have contacts, Mori, from many corners of the world, quite honestly. And I used them."

"Why TAKA?"

"Because despite the fact that your company is so traditional that there are no women in senior management, TAKA is still the best in the industry. Your assets, your operating principles. And because I respected the leadership of TAKA's new CEO," she told him bluntly. Why not? What more damage could she do now? She'd already slept with the man, breaking all manner of ethical behavior. What was one more—one *last*—revelation between them?

"You investigated TAKA."

"I investigated *you*. And don't pretend to be shocked. We both know that you investigated me, as well."

"Had my people done a better job, the existence of Jenny Anderson would not have come as such a surprise."

She wasn't amused and couldn't pretend to be.

"You are cannier than I realized," he finally said.

"A trait I'm sure you will never be able to appreciate."

"You think, because of my culture, that I do not understand shrewd behavior?"

"Shrewd, yes. Secretly manipulative? Probably not."

"You did this to save your late husband's company."

"We've been over that point already. Now, if you'll excuse me." She started to bow, but he caught her shoulders.

"Do not patronize me, Helen."

Was he so oblivious that he couldn't recognize that she was dying by slow degrees? "*Sumimasen.* That was not my intention. I just want to get through the next few weeks, Mori. That's all."

"And us?"

"As you've made plain to me, there is no *us* to concern myself with."

"Because I do not acknowledge you in front of my associates."

"That's just it, Mori. I don't need you to tell them that something important has occurred between us. But I don't want you hiding the fact even from me! Don't treat me as if I don't exist in that conference room. I won't ever be involved again with a man who cannot bring himself to acknowledge my value in a business setting."

She looked around them, profoundly grateful for the fact that, at that hour, there were only a few patrons in the place, and they looked three sheets to the wind. "I won't do that to myself again. I *can't*. And I'm sorry if you can't understand why that is so important to me. So all I can say now is…good night." When she moved, he released her, which was a good thing because she wasn't sure what she'd have done had he not.

Bursting into tears wasn't an acceptable action, even if she felt like she'd earned having one darned good howl.

The elevator that opened directly into the lounge was waiting, doors wide and she stepped on, turning to face outward.

Mori hadn't moved.

He stood where she'd left him, his expression closed.

She pushed the button for her floor and the doors slid shut.

Only then did she blink.

A hot tear slid down her cheek.

"Messages and mail for you, Hanson-san."

Helen headed for the reception desk and the smiling young woman who'd called out for her. She took the stack. *"Domō arigatō."*

The girl smiled and nodded. "It is my pleasure, Missus. Please enjoy your morning."

If only.

Helen slid the items inside her portfolio and followed Jack out into the morning sunshine. David, Evan and

Andrew were there, waiting, also. On this, the last scheduled meeting for the merger, they would all also be attending the meeting.

By the end of the day, the merger would be complete. Signed, sealed and delivered.

And Mori hadn't spoken privately with her since the night nearly two weeks earlier when he'd tracked her down in the cocktail lounge.

She felt a cowardly urge to hang back, to join Samantha and the other women for their day of playing tourists while the men bellied up to the bargaining table.

A limo was already waiting at the curb. "What are the messages for?" Jack asked. If he was aware of her nerves, he gave no hint.

She didn't look at the slips clenched in her hand. "The voice mail on my phone isn't working properly. I'm sure it's just stuff from Sonia."

He didn't ask any further questions and she climbed into the vehicle. Since the day they'd argued, he hadn't brought up the subject again. She supposed his uncommon reticence was probably Samantha's influence. She didn't care where it came from as long as it came. She didn't have any more stamina to keep facing Mori without losing her composure *and* stay firm against Jack's open censure.

She found herself sitting next to Jack and David, facing Evan and Andrew.

"We only have three points left to cover." Jack was looking out his side window. His fingers drummed against his knee. "One of which is the corporate philanthropy issue."

"I suppose you think I should just let them cut the

corporate match to whatever they want." She looked at the other men, waiting for some response.

"No." Jack's voice held a wealth of impatience. "But the sixty that Mori has already put on the table isn't completely out of the question."

Andrew nodded. Evan just looked distracted.

"What do you think, David?"

"If they'll go to sixty, they'll go up."

"That's what I think, too. I want seventy-five," Helen said.

"You should have been a defense lawyer," Jack muttered.

"Given the circumstances, I'll take that as a compliment." Whether he'd meant it as one, or not.

He snorted softly.

Helen opened her portfolio and glanced through the messages and mail.

Judge Henry had finally sent the letter.

She glanced at Jack from the corner of her eye, but he was still looking out the window. She discreetly slipped open the envelope, reading through the Judge's brief handwritten note. It accompanied another, smaller sealed envelope for Jack.

Satisfied, she tucked the second envelope in a pocket in the portfolio to save for later and continued paging through the messages. "Jack, I know the whole family is having dinner together tonight, but I was hoping to grab a few minutes of time with you and Evan."

Her middle stepson looked across at her. "Why?"

"There're a few things I want to talk with you both about." She closed her portfolio just as the taxi stopped in front of the TAKA building.

Evan's eyes narrowed. "What things?"

Sometimes he was *so* much like Jack, a fact he would undoubtedly deny. Adamantly, since he considered himself far less rigid than his older brother.

"It'll wait," she dismissed smoothly. "Jack, remember, seventy-five percent. You can argue it, if you like. I know how you like to do that."

"Well, that's the truth," Andrew agreed drily.

The men all eyed each other, half smiles on their faces.

She took in a slow, deep breath and let it out.

Everything was going to be fine. Just fine.

After dozens of meetings, the security guards had become familiar faces. Helen smiled and greeted them by name as she passed them for the elevator.

"You do have a way with people," Andrew muttered as they climbed on the elevator.

As they rode up, Helen was too nervous to worry whether Andrew's comment was a compliment or a condemnation.

When they walked into the conference room, Mori, typically, had not yet arrived. But Richard was already there and they joined him by the tea tray.

Anticipation seemed to hover, thick and heady, in the air.

"There are going to be a few board members here for this," Richard warned under his breath. "I overheard Shiguro talking about it."

Helen looked over to where Mori's younger brother was holding court with half a dozen other men. "Board members haven't joined any of the previous meetings."

"We haven't had the entire Hanson contingent here

at once, either. We're in the homestretch, kiddo."
Richard squeezed her elbow. "You done good."

She swallowed the knot of nervousness that continued rising in her throat despite her efforts otherwise.
Who was she kidding? She had an MBA and a decent
mind on her, with no real work history other than the
internship where she'd met George. The fact that she'd
gotten this far was a major miracle and she knew it.

Then Mori's father, Yukio, strode slowly into the
room. He was immediately surrounded by bowing
TAKA employees.

Her heart sunk to her toes. She turned slightly toward
Richard so that only he would hear her whisper. "Yukio
Taka is one of the board members coming today?"

"Kind of looks that way," he murmured, looking
around her at the man in question. "Guy walks around
like he's the emperor himself."

Helen turned again to face Yukio's direction and
decided it was an apt description. He was not as tall as
Mori, nor as broad in the shoulders, but his iron gray
hair was as thick as Mori's clipped hair. More than his
physical presence, though, it was Yukio's aging face
that caught at Helen.

It gave new meaning to the word *stern*.

And the look he was giving her would have probably
meant death in some previous century.

Even though she hated having to do it, she lowered
her lashes respectfully, put her hands on her thighs and
bowed deeply. When she raised up again, she liked to
believe she caught a glint of surprise in the man's eyes.

But the moment was too brief to be certain, and then
Mori entered the room.

He nodded at his father and went to the head of the table, his motions uncommonly brisk. "Shall we begin?"

Everyone quickly moved to the table and assumed their seats. Yukio sat directly across the table at the far end from his son. Moments later, two other elderly men shuffled into the room and took the two empty seats on either side of him. The other board members, she presumed.

Shiguro rose and introduced the TAKA visitors and then he sat down again, looking clearly rattled. While Richard stood and introduced Evan, Andrew and David, Helen looked past Jack to Mori.

He was watching her. She felt her cheeks warm and reminded herself just how easily the man had blocked out their personal relationship.

Then he spoke, seeming to direct his comment directly to her. "We will be brief today." A faint smile touched his lips and he finally looked around the table. "At least that is my hope."

A smattering of chuckles sounded. Helen glanced at the far end.

Yukio's expression had not changed.

She pulled out her gold pen, holding it tightly. The homestretch, she reminded herself. She could smell the barn.

Shiguro directed them to open their agreements to the suitable page. "The last remaining points, as we all remember, are the duration of the transitional management, the appointment of Hanson representatives to the TAKA board and setting policy for the philanthropic corporate match for Hanson North America."

There it was. No longer Hanson Media Group, but *Hanson North America.*

Helen stared hard at the pages in front of her and listened to Richard set forth their proposed timetable for the transitional management to ensure that all elements of the agreement actually took place. "While we realize TAKA would like to work through the transition as quickly as possible, we believe that a three-month period will be most feasible."

They'd begun requesting a five-month duration.

TAKA had wanted one month, but that was more noise than sense, and everyone was perfectly aware of it.

"Three months is acceptable," Mori agreed, cutting off any debate or discussion that might have occurred. He flipped open his leather-bound calendar. "January 30."

Everyone except Helen scribbled on their pages. She was busy watching Mori, wondering why he was suddenly being so agreeable.

"The appointment of board members has been reviewed." Shiguro moved to the next item. "Based on the list previously provided by Hanson."

They had only three seats, but those seats were permanent and as valuable as gold.

Helen had proffered the names herself, after some deep searching over what was best: Jack, Evan and David. She'd hoped to manage to get Andrew on the board, too, but TAKA had been inflexible about a fourth seat. Fortunately, Andrew hadn't taken the news too hard. He himself had seen the value of those chosen.

"The proposed board members are acceptable," Mori said, once again taking unilateral control.

"We are happy to hear that," Richard said.

Jack looked less satisfied. She knew he considered this just one more sign of his servitude to his father's company. But he'd had an opportunity to decline, and he hadn't. Which *she* considered one more sign of his true commitment to his family's heritage *despite* his father.

"As to the matter of the corporate match." Shiguro hesitated, looking from his brother to his father. "It is the position of TAKA that sixty percent remains the highest feasible amount."

Helen rolled her pen between her fingers. "With the consolidation of our scholastic divisions, as well as the additional seven percent cut in payroll, there is ample budget remaining for an eighty percent match. The additional twenty percent will remain under the control of Hanson Radio, which becomes a separate entity subsequent to the merger of the other divisions with TAKA Incorporated, and as such, is outside the bounds of this agreement."

"Silence!"

Helen nearly jumped out of her skin at the harsh command from Yukio. She looked toward him. "Excuse me?"

Both Jack and Richard touched their knees to hers beneath cover of the heavy conference table.

"*We* do not wish to hear from you, *gaijin.*"

Being ignored was one thing. Being chastised like an unwelcome child was another. "I am sorry for your displeasure, Taka-san," she said calmly, "but I *will* be part of this discussion."

Yukio stood. He folded his knuckles on the table and leaned forward. "Not while I have breath," he said flatly.

Helen looked toward Mori. His father may still hold a seat on the board, but Mori was the one in charge. His father had already tried to take control back from him.

Surely he would say *something* that would take the wind from Yukio's sails.

He was glaring at his father. "You do not have authority."

Yukio spoke sharply to his son in Japanese. By the reaction of the TAKA side of the table, he wasn't commenting on Mori's red tie. The two board members by his side looked uneasy, but they were nodding, clearly in agreement with whatever it was that Yukio said.

Mori's voice grew colder. "She *stays.*"

"My son—" Yukio looked around the table, finally speaking in English "—has been unfortunately influenced by *that*—" he hesitated "—woman."

Helen could feel things spiraling out of control.

"Oh, come on." Andrew looked disgusted. "Suck it up, Mr. Taka. We have."

Helen went still.

Andrew grimaced. "That didn't come out right, Helen. I didn't mean it the way it sounded."

She twisted the pen between her fingers. The pen that had been the only thing she could think of to give the man that she was married to, because he certainly hadn't been interested by then in anything of a more personal nature from her.

"Then what *did* you mean, Andrew?" Her voice was careful.

"Helen, now is not the time for this," Jack warned.

She turned and looked at him. "I don't know. Maybe this is the perfect time."

Even David and Evan looked uncomfortable.

And Mori…well, Mori wasn't saying a word, now.

He was just watching her. Always watching her with those all-seeing eyes of his.

Jack tilted his head closer to her, lowering his voice. "None of this would be happening if you could have kept your fingers off of Mori."

She looked down her side of the table at Jack's brothers. "Is that what you all think? That I'm only here for my *own* gain?"

"Helen," Richard cautioned, putting a hand over hers. "Remember where we are."

"As if I can forget." She slowly pushed back her chair and stood.

She'd given ten years of her life—willingly given them—to the Hansons. Believing in George's sons even when their own father had neglected them.

But even now, after everything that had happened since George had died, they couldn't at least offer the *appearance* of family unity. Not with her.

She stepped back from the table. "Helen," David protested. "What are you doing?"

"It's all right, David."

It wasn't, but that was entirely beside the point. It was nobody's fault but her own for having believed that she could get Hanson Media to this point and somehow gain the family that they'd never before been.

She pulled out the letter from Judge Henry from her portfolio and set it in front of Jack. "This will give you hope," she told him quietly. "That there is life again beyond this."

"What the hell are you doing?"

She didn't answer his furious demand. "Remember what I said. Seventy-five percent. Finish it, now."

Then she turned to Mori and bowed. "*O-jama shima-shita.* I am sorry to have disturbed you." She directed herself toward the opposite side of the table and bowed again. Finally, she faced Yukio Taka.

And though it galled, she managed to bow a final time.

Then leaving George's sons and brother behind, she walked out of the meeting.

And nobody stopped her.

Not Jack or Evan. Not Andrew or David.

Most particularly, not Mori.

Chapter Twelve

Silence reigned, thick and heavy, after the door slowly closed behind Helen's back.

Mori looked down the table at his brother and attorneys. "You will excuse us." He included his father's sidekicks in his request.

Shiguro looked regretful. He rose and the men silently left the room.

Yukio continued standing there and Mori had to struggle against his own anger with his father. "I will be speaking with the Hansons privately," he said.

Yukio glared.

Mori stared back. There were a lot of things he disagreed with his father about—in business and in life. But now was not the time for an argument over things that would always exist between them. They were simply too different.

Yukio finally made a disgusted sound and stomped out of the room.

A collective sigh seemed to escape Helen's family.

Mori studied them all for a moment. He moved around the side of the table and picked up the gold pen that Helen had left behind.

It sat on her open portfolio. The pad of paper beneath the pen was covered with her handwriting. The notes that she had been forever making to herself during their meetings.

He slowly closed the portfolio and slid the pen in his pocket.

"Perhaps it would be best to reschedule this for tomorrow," Richard suggested sensibly. "Give everyone a chance to cool off a little. Clearly, the stress of all this has gotten to us all."

"You heard Helen," Evan said quietly. "Finish it now."

Mori could see the silent debate being waged in the looks the men exchanged among themselves. "There is nothing to finish," he said, his voice flat.

Jack stood up like a shot. "Nothing to finish?" He lifted the corner of the merger agreement and let it drop heavily on the table. "I beg to differ, Mr. Taka. You've come too far to pull out now."

Mori moved around the table again until he faced them. "The night of your wedding—" he nodded toward Richard "—I observed to Helen that I believed her sons lacked honor. That they treated her with disrespect."

"We're not her sons," Andrew pointed out, his voice stiff.

"You are her family, nonetheless."

"Damn straight, we are," Evan said. "And we don't need you lecturing us about *our* family."

Mori almost smiled. So. There was more to them than he'd observed. "Helen strongly disagreed with me," he continued. "She insisted that her husband's sons had done nothing to be ashamed of. She spoke of all the Hansons with pride."

Jack tapped the edge of the envelope Helen had left him on the table. "We're not going to discuss Helen with you, Mr. Taka. Now, if you'd like to discuss the corporate pledge percentage, we can get this over with."

There'd been a time when Mori had used the Hansons' propensity for scandal to put the brakes on the merger. He had no regrets about that, still.

It was business.

But eyeing the men across from him, he knew it was no longer *only* business.

"Without Helen here, negotiations will not proceed."

"That's not what she wanted," Richard protested. "You heard her. Finish it."

"Are you certain that you know what Helen wants?"

"I suppose you think that *you* do?" Jack challenged. "What's she going to get out of this, Taka? Another decade of life with another guy who doesn't have time for her?"

"This is not about Helen and me," Mori assured. "This is about *you* and Helen."

"What? Unless we start acting like the adoring sons, you're not going to continue the deal?" Andrew stood. "How we feel about Helen is none of your damn business."

"I am making it my business. Do any of you have the first idea of all that she has done for you?"

"Well, her latest act is evidently putting the skids on the merger," Andrew said tightly.

"What do you mean, all she has done?" David asked slowly. "It was her idea to approach TAKA. We know that."

"It was her idea to have TAKA approach *you*," Mori corrected. "Had we not already become aware of Hanson Media's struggle and seen the value for ourselves of acquiring the company, we would not be here today."

"She manipulated it," Jack finished abruptly. He angrily tapped the envelope once more, then pushed away from the table and began pacing. "Just like she manipulates a lot of things."

"To what purpose does she do this?" Mori watched them all for a moment. When no answer was immediately forthcoming, he walked to the door and opened it. "When you can truthfully answer that and Helen is present for what she has every right to be present *for,* I will—perhaps—consider resuming our business relationship. Until then, we are finished." He barely inclined his head, he was so annoyed with the entire lot of them. *"Sayonara."*

Helen heard the knocking on her hotel room door but ignored it and continued fitting her clothes in the two suitcases opened on her bed.

Eventually, the knocking ceased.

She closed the first suitcase, zipped it shut and placed it on the floor in the living area. Then she returned to her packing.

Simple, methodical actions.

It was all she could concentrate on. If she let herself

think of the debacle she'd created, she would simply cease functioning altogether.

She went into the bathroom to collect her toiletries and caught a glimpse of herself in the mirror. "Haggard, Helen," she murmured. "Don't much look like George's sexy trophy wife now, do you?"

Her small perfume bottle escaped her blind reach and clattered into the sink. It shattered.

She sighed and grabbed a thick hand towel to scoop up the mess. She dumped the entire bundle in the tiny trash can and went back to the sink to rinse the strong perfume away. A swirl of red made its way down the drain, too. She'd cut her finger. Not badly enough to cause real pain, but enough to let a few drops of blood run.

She stuck her hand under the faucet and George's diamond ring winked up at her as water flowed over it.

She'd only been a Hanson because she'd been George's wife. And George was gone.

She turned off the water.

The ring slid off easily.

She set it on the sink and slowly dried her hands.

Her finger had already stopped bleeding.

She left the ring and went back to finish her packing. She hoped she'd be able to catch a flight back to the States without too much delay.

Hanging around the airport waiting any longer than necessary held little appeal.

"What are you doing?"

She gasped and whirled around, startled out of her wits.

Mori stood in the bedroom doorway.

"How did you get in?"

He held up a key card. "You are packing."

"They just *gave* you a key to my room at the front desk?"

"So it appears. You are running away?"

Her jaw tightened. She turned back to her suitcase and dropped her toiletry bag inside. "I prefer to think of it as going *home*."

"To your husband's house."

Her vision blurred. She blinked hard and reached for the suit she'd exchanged for jeans and a sweater when she'd gotten back to her hotel after walking out of the meeting. "Where else?" she asked flippantly. "No reason to hang around here. You men can handle everything most admirably, after all. No need for me to keep getting in the way, making things awkward for everyone. Just assure me that my guys got at least seventy-two percent out of you."

"Your *guys,* as you say, got nothing. I stopped the meeting."

She dropped the skirt and turned to face him. "Why would you do that?"

"You should not have left as you did."

"What was the point of staying? To be the cause of more dissension between you and your father? To have everyone on my side of the room blame me for that, as well?"

"Is that the true reason you left?"

"Why else?"

He frowned and shook his head. "Some days I wish I had never heard of Hanson Media Group."

"Then you'd be missing out on the best opportunity to gain a market share in North America," she countered immediately.

His lips twisted. "You still defend your company like a mama tiger."

"It's not my company. It is my husband's sons' company."

"Choosing to think of it that way is your prerogative, but that does not make it a fact. There will be no merger unless you are there until the last, Helen. And that is why I stopped the meeting."

"Jack and the others were working on my authority. They could have—"

"No."

She pressed her hands together. "You cannot possibly call off the merger at this late stage. It would be a public relations nightmare for TAKA. You've invested too much time and too much money."

"I could, Helen." His voice wasn't grim. It was factual. "Yes. It would create some inconveniences for us to overcome when next I venture into the North American market. But we both know that Hanson Media stands to lose far much more than does TAKA."

Her stomach was tipping over. She badly wanted to sit. "What is it that you want, Mori?" The last time she'd asked him that, he'd admitted he'd wanted *her.*

"I want two days of your time."

She felt like shaking her head to jar loose whatever was stuck inside. "For what?"

"An...experiment."

She finally gave up on appearances and sank down on the foot of the bed before her wobbling knees gave way. "Experiment for what?"

"To see if we can exist for even that amount of time without TAKA and Hanson Media Group."

He was speaking English, but it might as well have been Japanese. "I don't understand."

"Two days. You, a woman. Me, a man. No business. Nothing but us."

As quickly as it had turned somersaults, now her stomach was tightening. "You can't be serious. We were ten minutes away from signing the deal."

"Until you walked out."

"I walked out because it was clear that my presence was a hindrance!"

"That is a matter of opinion that not everyone shares."

"Well, I know you're not referring to my stepsons. And *you* didn't offer a dissenting opinion when your father was giving me a look that could have killed. When he was saying whatever it was that had everyone in the room who understood him looking at me with *pity!*"

"You wanted me to defend your presence to my father."

She knew it sounded infantile. That it made her sound like her ego was ruling her, that her pride was having a temper tantrum.

But it wasn't any of that.

It was the very basic root of self-esteem that she'd let wither on the vine as George's wife. It was finally back in bloom again, and to let it die would be to doom herself to a life of knowing that she was exactly what everyone had been saying—a pretty little trophy, of no use other than to decorate the arm of a man.

"What will two days prove?"

"That remains to be seen."

Which told her exactly nothing. She didn't need two days with the man to know that she'd done the unforgivable. She'd let him get under her skin where she'd never get rid of him.

"I could agree to this and you would never know if I was doing it for the sake of the merger."

He stepped forward and caught her chin in his, lifting it until their gazes met. "I would know."

She swallowed. Yes. He probably *would* know.

She shifted, lifting her chin away from his touch, and stood, putting several feet of distance between them. She'd thought alcohol clouded her senses, but Mori clouded her entire ability to think straight. "What did you have in mind? A two-day cooling off period or something?"

"This is not about the merger."

"Everything is about the merger."

"Maybe in the next few days you will learn that is not true."

"Then what?"

"I wish to take you to Nesutotaka. We can be alone there."

She locked her knees. "That's your home."

"Hai."

"You…want to take me to your home."

"Do you need it in writing? Yes. My home. We will have privacy there. No interruptions."

"I think if you go home, you should take your daughter, not me."

"Would you prefer to have her with us? A twelve-year-old chaperone?"

"Maybe."

"You do not have to sleep in my bed, Helen, whether Kimiko joins us or not."

"For a man who often dances politely around a topic, that's pretty blunt."

"I *hope* that you will choose to sleep in my bed," he allowed. "But you have a choice. You always do."

"She probably has school classes."

"Hai."

"If I said I wanted her to go with us, you would take her out, anyway?"

"Hai."

She tilted her head, studying him. "Even though my dreaded American ways might rub off on her during that time."

"How many ways do I say *yes?*"

"All right," she said abruptly. "Two days. And then we come back and you sign on the dotted line."

"And Kimiko? Do I call her headmaster?" He moved toward the phone as he spoke.

Helen bit her lip. She was charmed by Mori's daughter and the idea of the young girl's company was more than appealing. But she knew a portion of that appeal was because of the barrier Kimiko would provide between her and Mori.

"No," she said huskily. "I'll go with you. Alone."

He nodded. "Do you have a smaller suitcase that you can use? You will not need all of that." He gestured toward the suitcase still on the bed.

"You want to leave right *now?*"

"We will stop by my hotel only briefly. We will be in Nesutotaka by lunchtime if we leave now."

"Jack and everyone else must be furious."

"I am not concerned with them right now."

"I...okay." Proving what a weak-willed soul she was, she couldn't even summon another protest. "I don't have a smaller suitcase, but I've got a purse that ought to work." She rummaged through what she'd already packed and pulled it out. "I can't just leave, though. I've got to let them know where I'm going."

"Then make your calls," he said. "But if you delay too long, I suspect you will soon have more visitors."

She thought about that for a long moment. Sooner or later she'd have to deal with them. But at the moment, *later* seemed the more appealing choice.

She opened the empty hobo-style purse and dropped her toiletry bag inside. "I'll hurry," she told Mori.

"Pack those tennis shoes. Or wear them. You will need them."

She didn't ask why. She already felt like she was doing what he'd accused—running away. What was more appropriate than wearing running shoes on her feet when she did it?

Three hours later, as they drove into the village of Nesutotaka, Helen knew Mori hadn't exaggerated in his description of it as a collection of houses spread along a dirt road at the base of a mountain. What it looked like to Helen, though, was an oasis of simpler life set in the jewel tones of miles and miles of lush, green farmland.

She turned to Mori. The uncertainty over what they were doing had abated somewhat during the drive. "It's beautiful."

He smiled faintly.

He'd chosen to drive them to Nesutotaka himself, rather than take the car and Akira, his driver. The sports car was exorbitantly expensive and very eye-catching. Not at all what Helen might have expected of the man.

It also had them sitting for the drive from Tokyo extremely close.

She didn't have the heart to fake a complaint about it when the truth was that his nearness was as much a pleasure as it was a consternation.

The moment his car made its slow way along the bumpy, rutted road, word clearly spread that he'd arrived in the village.

Children, men and women suddenly appeared out of their houses, walking directly toward the road, waving their hands and greeting him by name.

Finally, he simply stopped right there in the center of it all, and rolled down his window.

Helen watched, entranced despite herself, as he laughed and spoke to everyone who tucked their head low enough to peer into the window.

She could only smile and nod as they eyed her and chattered rapidly and grinned and nodded in return. "They say you look like a movie star," Mori told her when they finally started moving again.

"A movie star?" She made a face. "No, that would have been my *former* look."

"You are not allowed to think right now of the man who was your husband," Mori told her. He closed his hand around hers and set it on his thigh. "It is only you and I here, remember?"

She was excruciatingly aware of the physique beneath her hand. But if he would act casually about it, then so could she.

She turned and looked through the rear window. There was still a cluster of people standing in the road, watching their progress. "Yes, just you and I," she agreed. "And a village that clearly delights in your presence. I suppose you know most of them?"

"I know all of them. They are all cousins in one way or another. Either on my mother's side, or my father's."

She turned back around. "You're kidding."

"Unfortunately, no." His assurance was arid. "We will stop and greet my mother, and then go on to my home."

She nodded, still distracted by the notion of possessing so many relatives. He'd already warned her they would visit his mother. "I don't have even one cousin," she told him. "Both of my parents were only children, born to their parents who were only children."

"I'm certain that if you went far enough back, you would find cousins exist."

"Sure. Distant ones whom I've never met and wouldn't know if I tripped over."

He looked amused. "Would you like to be an honorary cousin of mine?"

She shook her head, eyeing his lips for a moment. "No, thanks."

His lips curved faintly. "I thought not."

The car was moving at the bracing speed of— perhaps—five miles an hour and she was suddenly impatient to be alone with him in his home.

The strength of that particular yearning was still vaguely shocking to her.

Yes, she'd loved George. But—

No thoughts of George.

"Thank you for bringing me here," she whispered softly to Mori.

"Thank you for coming with me." He leaned forward suddenly and brushed his lips over hers, and then, when

the car bounced harder than usual, they pulled apart.
"This road is almost needing to be graded again."

"Almost?" She shook her head and laughed.

His dimple appeared.

After passing another half dozen homes and other un-
identifiable structures that she supposed were used as
barns for the cattle and goats that grazed, he turned off
the road onto an even more unbeaten track. But that path
was short and in moments, he'd pulled to a stop in front
of a house that had an ancient pickup truck and a luxury
sedan parked on the grass, as well.

Mori eyed the sedan. "My father is here," he said, all
of the humor now gone from his face.

Uncertainty came back with a nauseating vengeance.
"Did you tell him you were coming here?"

"No."

There was no point suggesting that he not go in.
She knew he wouldn't avoid seeing his father, even if
he wanted to. "I'll wait in the car." It seemed the wisest
choice.

The senior Mr. Taka loathed her on the business field;
she could only imagine how he'd feel seeing her here
now with his eldest son. Undoubtedly, he'd be on the
phone immediately, calling for another board meeting.

"No. You will come inside with me."

"Mori, why give your father more ammunition?"

"My father has no need for ammunition and he will
not dishonor a guest in his wife's home. Trust me. My
mother is expecting us." He squeezed her hand and
pushed open his car door. "She will not share my
father's opinion."

Helen wasn't all that certain of that. Not when she

was far more accustomed to having the family of the man she was involved with barely tolerating her presence. "What do you mean that your father has no need for more ammunition?"

"He and I resolved matters before I came to your hotel. Now, please. Come inside with me."

Clearly, Mori had no intention of sharing with her just *how* he'd resolved matters with Yukio. And she wasn't going to argue with him over the issue.

She reached behind her seat for the gift she'd brought for Mori's mother in the spare minutes she'd had while Mori had packed his own belongings. "How can you be sure your mother won't share your father's assessment?" she asked when he came around the car to help her out onto the uneven grass.

He touched her cheek, then took her hand and led her to the house. "She will see that I am happy to be with you," he said simply.

Her heart squeezed.

Maybe she wasn't making the biggest mistake of her life, after all.

As was typical, Mori did not knock on the front door, but slid it open, calling a greeting as they stepped into the *genkan.*

"You can leave your shoes here." He stepped out of his own street shoes, and then stepped directly onto the gleaming wood floor that was about half a foot higher than the ground-level floor where they'd entered.

She followed suit, being careful not to touch her stockinged feet to the *genkan* floor, knowing that would be bad form, as it might track dirt into the house, thereby defeating the purpose of the entry in the first place.

Two pairs of soft ivory slippers were waiting on the house level and they pushed their feet into them before walking along a short hallway that opened into a surprisingly large living area.

Given the traditional nature of the house up to that moment, Helen had expected tradition to continue in the living room. But instead of reed-mat flooring, low tables and floor cushions, there were Western-style couches, chairs and an enormous grand piano in one corner. It was a very comfortable, lived-in room that Helen found appealing.

The sight of Mori's father sitting like some royal entity in a large chair in the far corner of the room was considerably less appealing.

Thank goodness they'd had warning of his presence by the sight of his car outside.

Helen bowed slightly, acknowledging his presence. He, however, pretty much ignored her.

That was fine. It was certainly better than his open animosity.

Mori's mother—she could be no other—entered the room from another doorway, her small face wreathed in smiles and a very direct contrast to her husband's countenance.

"Mori-chan," she cried, grabbing him practically by the ears as she tugged his head down to kiss his face. She spoke rapidly in between hugs and kisses.

"English, Mama," Mori told her when she took a breath. "This is my friend, Helen Hanson."

"Friend," a deep voice repeated the word caustically.

Mrs. Taka shot her husband a quick look, which seemed to make the man subside in his chair. Then she turned to Helen and bowed deeply. "It is a great pleasure to meet my son's friend," she said carefully. "Welcome to our home."

Helen bowed, too. "*Domō arigatō gozaimasu.* Thank you very much. I am very pleased to meet you, too." She extended the basket of fresh flowers and tissue-wrapped pastries that she'd selected from the kitchen at her hotel. In this case, it had definitely paid to be who she was. The manager of the hotel had been incredibly eager to assist her.

"I hope you'll enjoy these," Helen told the woman.

"So pretty," the older woman said, lifting the blooms to her nose. "Thank you." She turned suddenly toward her husband. "*O-jii-san.*" Her tone sharpened and the man frowned mightily at her. A frown over which Mrs. Taka seemed to take little offense and the man finally stood.

"Please to be seated," he told Helen and Mori, his English stiff and cold.

Helen wasn't sure *which* seat she was supposed to take, but Mori solved the problem by taking her hand— which earned another eagle-eyed look from Daddy— and leading her to the couch nearest them.

Mrs. Taka was nodding her pleasure and she excused herself after a moment, returning almost immediately with a beautiful wooden tray full of refreshments which she set on the low ebony table in front of them.

Instead of sitting on one of the chairs, however, she kneeled down, sitting on her folded legs next to the coffee table. "You had a good travel?"

"*Hai,*" Mori answered. "Traffic was light. We made good time. Arrived here earlier than I had anticipated."

He looked at his father. "Apparently, earlier than anyone had anticipated."

Helen kept her focus on the welcoming demeanor of Mori's mother. "Mrs. Taka, Nesutotaka is every bit as lovely as Mori described. You grew up here?"

"My family has been here for generations. I find the busyness of the cities—" she hesitated, searching for the word she wanted "—chaotic. My son has told me you live in Chicago."

"Yes. And it, too, can be chaotic."

"But your family is there?"

"My stepsons and their families. Well, Jack, the eldest, is in Tokyo now because of the merger."

Mr. Taka muttered something that Helen felt relieved not to hear clearly. Mori replied, his voice equally low.

"Do you speak Japanese?" Mrs. Taka asked.

"Regrettably, only a little." Helen lifted her hands slightly, palms turned up apologetically. "I am learning, but not as quickly as I'd like."

"You have intelligence," Mrs. Taka said. "My son has told me this. You will learn in time."

Helen flicked a glance at Mori, sitting beside her. His entire body was tense, and concern for that almost overrode her quiet pleasure that he'd told his own mother that she was intelligent.

"Mori-chan." Mrs. Taka turned her focus on her son. "When will you bring my granddaughter to see me?"

"In a few weeks, Mama. She'll have a break from school, then."

"I miss my granddaughter," Mrs. Taka told Helen. "I do not see her often enough. Each time, she has grown much between visits."

"She is a lovely girl." Helen smiled. "Her English, as yours is, was much better than my Japanese."

The woman laughed a little. "Kimiko is a challenge to her father, but I delight in everything she does."

"I think that's the right of grandparents."

"Your pretty Hanson-san is very correct," Mrs. Taka told Mori. "You will tell Kimi-chan that she can bring her favorite movies to share with me on my new television."

"Mama, you have a TV?"

"*Hai.* Your father made me a gift of one even though I told him I did not want it. He has a liking for the American football," she divulged.

Helen couldn't have been more surprised. She'd believed that Mr. Taka had a disliking for everything American. Maybe it *was* just her he detested.

"The satellite doesn't always work," Mrs. Taka was saying, "but he is content when he is here."

"Speaking of contentment—" Mori set down his cup and stood "—that is what I seek for the next few days. So, you will please excuse us. We will stop by again before returning to Tokyo."

Helen hid her relieved surprise at the abruptness of Mori's announcement, and stood as he kissed his mother's cheek and exchanged a few words with his father.

Mrs. Taka accompanied them out to the foyer where they exchanged their slippers for their street shoes and walked out into the cool afternoon. Helen felt as if she towered over the diminutive woman as she bowed and thanked her for her hospitality. The woman stood there, watching, until she and Mori drove away from the house.

Helen was silent until they turned back onto the main track. "Doesn't your father think he's won, given the fact that we didn't sign the papers this morning?"

"No." He cast Helen a sideways glance. "And now, we put all talk of TAKA and Hanson Media out of doors. We are just a man and a woman. Remember?"

She bit the inside of her lip. That had been a fantasy—one that would be nearly impossible to realize. But for these few days, she would give it her best effort and not think about the hell to pay when they returned to Tokyo and the people who were waiting in a holding pattern. "I remember."

He squeezed her hand then pointed through the windshield at the mountain. The closer they drew to it, the more she realized the car was climbing.

"We will watch the sunrise from the top of that peak," he told her.

She pressed her lips together, eyeing the peak in question. The mountain was not as imposing as it could have been, but it was *still* a mountain. "And how do we *get* to the top of that peak?"

His dimple appeared. "We climb, Mrs. Hanson. How did you think?"

"I don't know." She leaned forward, peering through the window. "Helicopter?" she said hopefully.

"What is the challenge in that?" he said, amused.

"Exactly." But as long as he had that sexy half smile on his face, she knew she'd agree to nearly any sort of mountain climbing.

"You realize—" she cast him a sidelong look "—that if I'm to get to the top of that peak by sunrise, that I'll have to have an early night tonight."

"That was my plan." He suddenly stopped the slow progress of the car, putting it into Park right there in the center of the path. "We're here."

Helen looked around them. All she could see was the village slightly below them and the side of the mountain. "Are we camping out?"

His grin widened and he pushed out of the car. She didn't wait for him to come around and open her door and climbed out, too. He'd popped the trunk and pulled out his small bag and her somewhat larger impromptu overnighter-purse. "Come with me." He walked ahead of the car several yards.

And then she saw the iron gate that opened right off the road. He pushed it open to reveal stone steps leading even farther up the hill.

"I feel like I'm entering a sanctuary," she told him as she preceded him up the steps.

"Now you understand why I come here."

"I understand why you're in great shape," she said, lifting her chin at the dozens of steps that lay before them. "This is all part of the hike to get to that peak, right?"

He laughed softly. "Keep going, Helen."

She groaned, but did as he bid. At least she was wearing her tennies. If she'd had to ascend these stairs wearing her typical high-heeled pumps, she'd be lame by the time she reached the top.

Her breath was short by the time the steps leveled out in a clearing that fronted the beautiful wood house. A very *modern*-looking house. "Well." She stopped, smoothing her hand down her ponytail. "I guess I don't have to ask if this house has been in your family for generations."

"I built it after my wife died."

So, his arranged wife had never been inside the walls. She didn't like the relief that she felt over that particular fact. It seemed petty and small.

But she still felt it.

"And you found some peace here?"

"I always find peace here." He took her hand and led her toward the house.

The front sliding door was unlocked and opened at his touch. "There is no need for security here. The only way here is through the village."

"Who would notice any strangers, I suppose. What about by air?"

"There is no place to land. An intruder would have to rappel or parachute from the craft, which takes at least a few minutes. They would still be noticed. Besides, nothing here is related to TAKA. A person who thinks otherwise will be very disappointed."

The exterior of the house was far more updated than that of his mother's, but it still possessed a similar vestibule where he toed off his shoes before stepping up onto the elevated main floor. "I will get you slippers," he told her, and disappeared beyond a short hall.

She removed her shoes and stepped up onto the wood floor, looking around her curiously as she followed the direction he'd taken. The first room she came to was everything that she'd expected his mother's living area to be. Reed-mat floors. One low, central table. Brilliant red cushions stacked against a wall.

Though there was a wealth of deep, gleaming wood, the sense of the place was still airy and light. Many tall, narrow windows closely placed together afforded an expansive view of the village below.

"It is not what you expected." He came up behind her and slid his arm around her waist.

She closed her eyes for a moment against the rush of desire that hit her. "You're never quite what I expect, Mori."

"That is good in business. Is it good in personal matters?"

She threaded her fingers through his where they rested on her hip. "In this personal matter, I'd have to admit I have no complaints." She pressed her head back against his shoulder, looking up at him.

She felt like Alice, having fallen down the rabbit hole, so odd did it seem to be there with him when just that morning they'd been at the bargaining table. "I...I haven't felt like this before, Mori."

"This?" His eyes were hooded, his voice low.

She didn't know how to answer. "This passion," she finally settled on. "I know it probably seems unlikely at my age, but—" She broke off when he touched his forefinger to the corner of her mouth.

"Turn your frown upside down," he murmured with a smile. "Does passion have an age limit?"

She turned in his arms, finally pushing out all other thoughts but of him. She looped her hands around his neck. "I certainly hope it doesn't."

"My grandfather was ninety-two when he died. He told me once that the secret to his long life was not his harmony with the world around him, but the warmth of the woman who lay beside him every night."

"Your grandfather really told you that?"

"My grandfather taught me what matters in life," he murmured. His mouth touched the point of her chin, then the spot directly below her ear.

She dropped the slippers he'd handed her. "Mori?"

He tugged on her ponytail, tilting her head back. "Yes?"

"We don't have to wait until nighttime, do we?"

"What do you think?" She felt the smile on his face when he closed his mouth over hers.

Then he lifted her right in his arms and carried her to his room.

Reality, Helen thought hazily, as he placed her on his low bed, was sometimes even better than the dream.

Chapter Thirteen

Mori hadn't been joking about watching the sun rise.

Helen shivered as she pulled on the thick ivory fisherman's sweater he tossed across the bed to her. A small table lamp was lit in the dark room. The only other illumination came from the glow of the spectacular fish tank built into one of the walls. Mori was already dressed in jeans and a dark blue sweater and the house smelled of coffee.

The scent had her salivating, and the sight of him had her fumbling with the sweater as she dragged it over her head. "I thought you didn't *drink* coffee," she said when her head poked through.

"You do."

Her hands tightened on the jeans she was pulling out of her overnight bag. He'd fixed coffee just for her?

"Smells wonderful," she told him huskily.

He smiled a little and headed back out of the room. "Hurry. We have only forty-five minutes before sunrise. Then we will return and cook breakfast."

Helen dragged on her jeans, looking somewhat long-ingly at the comfortable bed. She didn't doubt the beauty of the sunrise Mori was determined to share, but couldn't he find something interesting to occupy him-self with if they remained in bed?

He'd certainly had no trouble in that regard through-out the night.

When she was finished dressing, she quickly cleaned her face and teeth and dragged her hair into a ponytail. Then she headed out to the kitchen that—contrary to the traditional nature of his living area—provided every convenience known to man.

He stuck a stainless steel travel cup in her hand and aimed her toward the *genkan* where he crouched at her feet. "Lift."

Pouring the coffee down her throat, she lifted her foot. He stuffed it into her tennis shoe and tied it and repeated the process.

She wanted to giggle, but squelched it in her coffee mug.

He pulled on his own shoes, much sturdier looking than her pristinely white court shoes, and then nudged her out the door.

The air was cold enough to make her suck in her breath, and wish she hadn't. "Mori, wouldn't you rather be in that wonderful, soft bed of yours, all warm and cozy?"

He closed his hand over her shoulder and flipped on a small flashlight, shining the beam over the ground in front of her. "It will be worth it."

She hugged her arms closer, hunching over the coffee mug. "Better be," she mumbled. "I don't get up at this hour for just anyone, you know."

"Then I am deeply honored." His tone, however, told her he was deeply amused. "You will be glad for the climb, Helen. Never will you have a better morning than after you have seen these mountains."

They walked beside each other for several minutes, then Mori took the cup from her hands and replaced it with the flashlight. "Go first."

She looked longingly at the gleam of stainless steel. It still had a healthy measure of steaming hot coffee inside. "How about if you let me carry my coffee and I follow you?"

"You do nothing without a debate, do you?"

"Well." She tilted her head and smiled slightly. "There are a few things with you I haven't debated."

He laughed softly. "True. I am most aware of that. Now, go before me."

"Why?" She swept the beam of the flashlight ahead of her, seeing what—to her—looked like a straight, upward shot. "So if I fall on my rear end, you can catch me?"

"Perhaps I will just be enjoying the view."

She choked back a surprised snort. "Morito Taka, you have a naughty mind."

"You have a delightful derriere that inspires me. Now, move. There is a path. You will see when you start heading upward."

Biting her tongue to keep from laughing, she went ahead of him. "I thought we'd been heading *upward*, all along." But the climb wasn't *quite* as difficult as she'd

feared. The path was visible. Just. It took most of con-
centration not to stray.

Around them, she could smell the biting scent of
vegetation and earth, and heard the occasional rustle of
something she figured she was glad not to see.

Mori surely heard it, too, and he wasn't the least
concerned so she took her cue from him.

The higher they went, the more her thighs felt the
pull of the ascent, the more grateful she was for the
cool air, since it wasn't long before she felt herself beginning to sweat. Clearly, her Pilates class wasn't going to cut the mustard if she were to make *this* climb
very often.

The thought sneaked in.

Her foot dragged over the loose dirt. The beam of
light bobbled in her hand.

Behind her, Mori's hand planted itself on the small
of her back, steadying her. "Are you all right?"

Where did she get the nerve to begin thinking that
this little diversion was likely to be repeated?

And why did she feel any sort of regret at the notion
that it wouldn't be?

"Helen?"

"Just swell," she puffed.

"We are nearly there," he assured.

She gestured with the flashlight. It was still pitch
dark beyond the glow of yellow light. "I'll have to take
your word for that, too."

"Do you think I would send you into harm?"

"No, but I think you might be sending me along the
garden path," she returned drily.

His hand on her back urged her gently forward. "The

sun will be up soon. The path will even out and widen a few yards ahead."

"Promises, promises." She forced her tired legs into motion. "I feel I must tell you that I am *quite* certain we have been climbing for more than forty-five minutes."

He chuckled. "Try about twenty-five minutes."

"You're slaughtering my ego here, Mori."

"My humble apologies." He stepped beside her, when the path widened, just as he'd promised. "I will trade you again." He took the flashlight and handed her the coffee mug.

When she took a sip, it was as piping hot as it had been before they'd set out. She let out an appreciative sigh. "How do you know how to make such good coffee when you don't even drink it?"

"I know how to operate a good coffee machine." He played the flashlight ahead of them. "We have one more little climb."

Just hearing the word *climb* made her thighs protest. "Seriously?"

"Come." He took her arm and led her forward. When he stopped, he let go of her and easily stepped up onto a high boulder. "Give me your hand."

The sky was just beginning to lighten. She looked up at the shadow of his outstretched hand and settled her palm on his.

The realization dawned on her as abruptly as a sliver of light began peaking over the horizon that she hadn't even realized she was facing.

She was in love with him.

"Helen?"

Shaking herself, telling herself not to be utterly ridiculous, she stepped up, feeling him nearly take her weight as he lifted her to the top of the boulder.

He led her forward again off the boulder and onto hard-packed earth, and then stopped. "We can sit here."

She nodded and sat down when he did, her numb attention focused on the darkening band of scarlet color stretching out in front of them for as far as she could see.

He shifted around until he sat directly behind her, pulling her back against his chest. "Warm enough?"

"Mmm-hmm." Was she out of her mind? George hadn't even been gone a year yet. She *couldn't* be in love with someone else.

Mori slid his arm around her waist, his hand flat against her belly through her thick sweater. "Now, you see why I brought you here?"

She made herself concentrate. The mountainside on which they sat faced away from the village. In the gradual lightening that bathed the view in cool, silvery light, she couldn't see a single mark of human hand. She pressed her lips together for a moment. "Yes, I see. I've never been anywhere like it." She balanced her mug on the ground beside them and folded her hands over his arm.

He closed his other arm around her, enclosing her in his warmth as the temperature seemed to drop. It was as if the energy of the emerging sun was sucking away at everything else.

His fingers threaded through hers. "You took off your wedding ring."

"Yesterday."

"I noticed at your hotel room."

"You didn't say anything."

"Nor did you."

Well, that was certainly true. She imagined the ring would still be sitting on the edge of the sink when they returned.

"Do you still think of yourself as married to him?"

"No. Yes." She rubbed her head against his chin. "Sometimes. When I'm with his boys, I tend to."

"When you are with me?"

That one was easy. "Not when I am with you." She relaxed even more against his chest. She could feel the even cadence of his breathing, and realized hers was slowing to match his.

It struck her suddenly as incredibly arousing.

She bit the inside of her lip, sternly redirecting her attention to the horizon. An undulating stripe of yellow had joined the gleam of scarlet. "Have you photographed this?"

"*Hai.*" His voice was low, a soft rumble against her ear that sent heat coursing through her.

"*Hai,* indeed," she murmured.

They were entirely alone. They could do anything they wanted, there on the mountainside.

She lowered her hands onto his thighs and unfolded her crossed legs, stretching them out, as his were. The tips of her tennis shoes barely reached his ankles.

Her fingertips flexed against his unyielding thighs. "Who else have you brought here?"

He laughed softly and pressed his lips against the side of her neck. "Only Kimiko," he assured. "We take a slightly different path and watch the sun set. She does not wish to be roused from her bed at an hour such as this."

"Well." Her head tilted back, giving him better access

to her throat. "I am beginning to see the—" she let out her breath when he kissed her neck again "—the, um, the appeal of *rousing* this early."

"I thought you might." His breath was warm against her ear when he spoke. "Are you cold?"

"Not at the moment." She reached up and caught her hand behind his neck, finding his mouth with hers.

His hands tightened on her and the satisfied sound he made rumbled along her spine as he briefly deepened the kiss. Too briefly.

"Open your eyes and watch the sunrise, Helen."

She dragged her eyes open. The silver cast had turned golden. The mountains around them were no longer mere shadows, but cool, purple peaks. A curve of the sun was nudging its head above a horizon that writhed with fiery tendrils of orange and pink and red.

This was seduction of the headiest kind, she decided. And as steadily as the sun began its rise, the emotion inside Helen gathered together. She was in love with Mori.

"See the sun? That is what it feels like when I hold you."

"You don't have to say things like that, Mori." Her throat was tight.

"I think I do." Not until he wiped his thumb down her cheek did she realize that tears had been leaking from her eyes. "You are unhappy?"

The sun was up. The brilliant colors were fading away. She would never again look at a sunrise without thinking of Mori. She shook her head. "I'm very happy. You were right. It was a magnificent sight. Thank you for sharing it with me."

"Forcing you to share it with me, you mean."

She smiled slightly. "*Force* might be a bit strong. I was willing enough."

He grinned. "When the coffee beckoned. Come." He kissed her hard on the lips. "We will now go down and have breakfast. The finest you will ever taste."

She pressed her palm against his cheek, slowing him for just a moment. "The finest *you* will ever taste," she returned huskily. She wasn't speaking of food.

The appreciative gleam that entered his deep brown eyes told her he was well aware of that fact.

And she was suddenly in a tearing hurry to get off the mountain and she scrambled inelegantly to her feet. "Come on. You were in a hurry to get up here. I'm in a hurry to get down there."

He rose and there was nothing ungainly about his movement. "I do not hurry. I am a man of patience."

"When you want to be," she allowed, slipping her hands beneath his sweater and loving the way his hard abdomen jumped a little at her touch. "When it suits you. Other times, you're like a freight train, charging through life."

His eyebrows drew together, creating a fierce dark slash across his striking face. "I am more careful than a mindless train."

She smiled. Flickered her fingers against his belly. He caught her fingers and she knew she'd found at least one secret where he was concerned.

The man was ticklish.

"Nobody said you were mindless, Mori." She stepped close to him, until barely a breath separated them. "You are a man of action." Her voice dropped. "Aren't you?"

She felt the tension that filled his body and with a

woman's instinct, knew that he felt the heat streaking through her, as well.

His gaze focused on he lips. After a long moment—long enough that Helen considered the dwindling likelihood that they might even make it off the mountainside before her control deserted her—he took a step back.

Oddly enough, the heat inside her only increased.

"Lead the way."

She swallowed. Picked up the coffee mug and headed back down the mountain, increasingly aware of his deliberate, sure steps behind her.

When they finally reached his house, they toed off their shoes. Mori wrapped his fingers around her wrist, starting to lead her through the kitchen, but she dragged her feet. "Too far," she whispered at his look when she slipped off her sweater and shook out her hair.

A faint smile grew around the corners of Mori's lips. "Who wishes to turn out a light now?"

She dragged his sweater up and off his head next. He had the most extraordinarily well-defined body she'd ever seen. Probably earned from activities like climbing that very mountain. Looking at him was almost as mind-boggling as touching him, she'd realized. "You have only yourself to blame."

His smile widened. "I will accept the responsibility."

"Such honor." She pushed him back until they met the very rustic and very substantial table that sat in the middle of the room. The warmth of his knuckles brushing against the button at her waist maddened her.

"This is the honor," he murmured. His hand drifted upward, sliding against the tiny center clasp of her bra. She moistened her lips, anticipation making her want to squirm. But he didn't unfasten it as his unreasonably light touch grazed over her breast, circling her nipple, which tightened even more for him. "Touching you."

A knot grew in her throat again. She wanted to tear off the rest of his clothes, to ravage him as thoroughly as his gentle, skimming touch ravaged her. "Touch more." Her plea was husky but she was too filled with need to care that she'd begged.

"Anything in particular?"

Her head felt heavy. She pressed her forehead against the satiny skin that hugged his broad shoulder and slid her hands from his waist, down his hips. "Everything," she sighed. "Oh, Mori. Everything. And hurry."

His breath drew in on a chuckle that was as much hiss as humor. "Impatient American." He reached between them, and her bra separated. She wanted to cry with delight when her bare flesh finally met his hard chest.

"That would be me," she agreed, smiling against him.

But it wasn't long before smiles turned to sighs and laughter turned to longing that could no longer be denied. She dragged at his jeans. He dragged at hers. The tabletop was cool, but the table legs were sturdy and Helen didn't care if she was shocking Mori or not. Because he was inside her again, and pleasure blasted through them both.

And Helen knew, once again, that her life would never again be the same.

By the time they finally started the meal, it was well past breakfast time. So she sat at the table she felt increasingly fond of and watched him fix their lunch, instead.

He'd never bothered to shut the door they'd left open

and a cool breeze occasionally blew through. She propped her elbows on the table and rested her chin on her hands as she watched him.

Morito Taka.

Barefoot.

He had *very* sexy feet, she decided lazily.

Fact was, he was very sexy from those feet all the way up to the top of his closely cut black hair.

He glanced at her occasionally as he chopped fresh vegetables and deftly filleted a salmon, all of which, he'd told her, had been delivered from the village while they'd been communing with nature. "What are you smiling at? I told you once that I enjoy the kitchen, did I not?"

"Well—" her lips curved "—at the time you told me that, I thought you were referring to *cooking*."

His grin widened.

"You just look good, that's all," she finished. "So I'm smiling."

His gaze lingered on her face for a moment. "You look good, also."

She certainly felt good. Hadn't felt so good in weeks. Months.

Years.

"I'm happy," she said finally.

"I am glad." He turned back to his preparations.

"What would you be doing if you weren't running TAKA?"

He shrugged. "I would not be *not* running TAKA."

"Use your imagination."

He shot her an amused look over his shoulder.

"You've already proven you're quite adept at that," she reasoned.

He popped a slice of red pepper in his mouth and seemed to contemplate the question as he chewed. "I would garden," he finally said.

She could have fallen off her chair. "Garden?"

He pointed the tip of his deadly-looking knife at the plants that grew in profusion outside the kitchen windows. "Garden. You have seen the one in my suite at the Anderson hotel."

"*You're* the one who takes care of that jungle?"

"Who did you think?"

She shook her head. "I don't know. The hotel, I suppose."

"No. I do. It is…satisfying."

He'd surprised her, yet again.

"What would you be doing if not for Hanson Media?"

"Having my hair or nails done," she said immediately. Then, at his long look, she shrugged. "I don't honestly know. For so long, I wanted to be a part of that side of George's life and he refused. I can hardly remember *not* wanting to be doing something there, even if it meant filing press clippings."

"What is it you like most?"

"I don't know. I haven't been involved in Hanson until recently. And since then I've been working on the merger."

"You like the hunt?"

She wrinkled her nose. "I don't know that I'd put it that way."

He laughed softly and tossed his peppers into the wok he'd placed on the stove.

"I think I'm not too awful at negotiations," she finally said.

He shook his head. "No, you are not awful at all."

She decided that was pretty high praise, coming from him. "Mori? How did you convince your father to back off?"

"Why?"

She studied the lines of his strong back as he tended the vegetables. Already the kitchen was fragrant with them and her stomach was growling so loudly, she feared he would hear. "How do you know he won't try to stop the merger yet again? He doesn't really want you to step down from TAKA, does he?"

"I will see that my father is voted off the board if he does."

She pressed her lips together, swallowing her shock.

Mori sighed a little and continued. "He wishes that he were still the head of that household. But he also knows his time there has passed. He struggles with that. Some day, that will be my struggle."

Helen couldn't honestly see Mori behaving the way Yukio had. "I'm not sure I could be as understanding if I were in your position," she said faintly.

"You do not have understanding for your stepsons?" His voice was dry. "You defend them even when you wish to throttle them."

"They're my family," she murmured. "And I don't usually wish to throttle them. Andrew, oh, he'll make such a great father when Delia has the baby. He'll bend over backward being exactly what his own father was not. If ever there was a playboy happy to trade it in for a woman, it's Andrew with Delia. Not that he started out feeling quite that way. And Jack will make an incredibly fair judge one day. Samantha is just enough of a free spirit to keep him from becoming *too* set in his ways."

"And Evan? He is not married."

"Not yet. It's only a matter of time, though. He and Meredith have been *it* for each other since they were in high school together. They've just needed some time to adjust to that particular fact. Evan's had the hardest time since his father's death. George completely cut him out of the will." She shook her head. "He refused to see Evan's potential. It was so wrong of him. Yet I know he was really quite proud of the way Evan never asked him for *anything*."

"What about your brother-in-law? He was not close to your husband?"

"Remember that David is considerably younger than George was. They hardly knew each other, really. David was mostly raised by nannies. If it weren't for Hanson Media, they would have probably been complete strangers."

"And then there is you. Who brings their focus together for the company."

"David already worked there before I came along."

"Do not downplay what you have done, Helen. I know the other three had nothing to do with Hanson Media until they had to." He set a plate of vividly colored stir-fried vegetables and flaking salmon in front of her.

"Which they can all blame me for," Helen said, striving for matter-of-factness and falling short. "They'd have come together without me, though, Mori. I still believe that. They'd have done what was necessary to save their heritage."

"So, you believe that about them when their own father told you in that letter that he did not."

"George shouldn't have underestimated his family

the way he did. But even he wanted them to have the company in the end, or he wouldn't have bothered writing that letter and leaving it for me to find. He knew I was the one person who wouldn't be able to ignore his request. He played on my feelings for him. If he truly didn't care about any of his sons, he wouldn't have done that."

She forked a piece of fish to her mouth and nearly groaned in pleasure as she ate it. "You know, if this chancy TAKA thing doesn't work out for you," she finally told him, "and the gardener thing falls through, you could definitely get a gig as a chef."

His eyes crinkled as he settled himself on the chair next to her with his own plate. "A comforting thought, indeed."

Helen grinned and tucked into her meal.

After, they washed the dishes together and drove into the village to call on his mother.

She insisted they stay the afternoon and have dinner with her.

Mori's father had returned to the city, she told them.

Helen, for one, was relieved.

Before long, additional people began arriving at the house until the living area was fairly bulging with them.

Helen even managed to converse with some of them in Japanese, and by the time the women began setting out dishes of food on a long table that Mori and some of his cousins set up, she'd even lost her nervousness about making some faux pas.

She was laughing over her fumbling attempts to pick up a burstingly plump shrimp with her chopsticks when she looked toward Mori, across and several seats down from her.

He lifted his wineglass in a silent toast.

Helen's amusement didn't fade, but a deeply satisfying contentment filled her.

Yes. She was happy. And she was not going to worry about how long that happiness was going to last.

For now, for this moment there with Mori and his amazingly boisterous and generous family, she had everything she'd ever wanted.

Chapter Fourteen

"Back to the real world." Helen looked through the window of Mori's car up at the exterior of the sky-high hotel. She had no idea what sort of welcome—or *un*welcome—she would receive.

And appealing as it was to think she could hide out with Mori, their escape had not been indefinite.

"I will go up to your room with you."

She turned to him and laid her hand along his jaw. She slowly kissed his lips. "Thanks, but no." She'd already told him she would face George's family on her own. "I don't need you distracting me," she added, not untruthfully.

"Pity. We distract each other well together."

She smiled and kissed him once more. Inside, however, she was nowhere near as calm as she let on. "I was thinking that I might stay in Tokyo for a while. You know. After the merger. I could take a leaf out of Samantha and Jack's book. They want to find an apartment or something a little more permanent than the hotel during the transition."

"Why would you want to remain in Tokyo?"

Everything inside her stopped cold at his question. Why?

Why?

Perhaps because she'd stupidly set aside common sense, once again?

Because she'd allowed herself to think beyond the moment, to contemplate some sort of future with both of them in it?

Because she'd believed him when he'd told her that not *everything* was about the merger?

Mori was watching her curiously, a faint line showing between his eyebrows at her protracted silence.

She made herself shrug. "It was just a thought," she finally said smoothly and though she wanted to pound her head against the window, she simply pushed open the car door and stepped out, grabbing her purse that she'd used for Mori's interlude. "You'll let me know when the meeting will be rescheduled?"

"Hai."

She nodded, smiled smoothly and turned on her heel, heading straight into the hotel.

She did not allow herself to look back.

"She's back." Samantha hung up the telephone and faced the others. "That was the concierge. He said Helen went up to her room about twenty minutes ago."

"High time," Jack said.

Samantha gave him a look and he made a face. She knew he felt badly about the way things had turned out.

"I just don't like sitting here cooling our heels while she's out—"

"Living *her* life for a few days?" Meredith put in. Nina, David's wife, sat beside her on the settee and she was nodding her agreement.

"Every one of you has said you never understood what the deal was between your father and Helen," Delia reminded. She sat in a chair, her hands folded over her very pregnant stomach. "Andrew says he thought his father always put Helen last."

"She could have done something about it," Jack argued.

Samantha went to him and slipped her arm through his. "Regardless of the dynamics of their marriage, Helen loved your dad."

"She sure hasn't grieved very long," Andrew murmured. "Going off with Taka like that."

Delia eyed him. "And what *is* the acceptable time frame for falling in love, Andrew?"

He looked back at her. She was nearly a decade older than he was, and he'd never been happier in his life than he was with her.

And Helen had encouraged their relationship.

He went over and sat on the arm of the chair next to his wife and kissed the top of her head. "Point taken."

Meredith looked across the room at Evan, who'd been pacing like some sort of anxious jungle cat. Evan, who was the most laid-back person she'd ever met. "Someone should call her. Have her come up here. Or we should go to her suite."

"Doesn't much matter where we meet," Evan said.

"Either way, we've got a pretty big helping of crow to choke down."

"It's the right thing to do," Jack said. He looked at his brothers, who nodded in turn.

David had picked up the letter from Judge Henry that had been sitting on the coffee table for the past few days where Jack had left it. "She was pretty smart to try and put you and Judge Henry together. When he retires next year, there's going to be a temporary vacancy on the bench that you might well be perfect for."

"I'd have preferred not to have it come about through my stepmother's manipulation," Jack countered.

"How is that any different than the connections your old law firm worked on? All she is doing is introducing the two of you," Samantha defended. "It's entirely up to you what comes out of it. The judge can't give you his old job, after all. You'll have to be appointed and then win an election to *keep* it. And you know you want to get back to the law so badly you can taste it."

He couldn't deny it.

"I think, if I'd been in her shoes," David said, "I'd have told us all to take a flying leap. She could have sold off her shares in Hanson and still made a fortune, despite the state the company was in."

"Suffice it to say that we have all underestimated her," Andrew conceded.

"Well, I know Helen from way back," Samantha said. "So I'm not the least surprised that she didn't cut her losses and run. That's not her—" she hesitated when they all heard a knock on the door "—way," she finished.

Evan, closest, opened the door.

Helen wasn't expecting to see Evan's face when the door to Samantha and Jack's suite was pulled open.

His gaze drifted over her appearance with some surprise.

"Yes," she said evenly, "Even I own jeans. May I come in?"

He jerked a little. "Sorry. Of course. You just look—"

She lifted her eyebrows, waiting.

"Tired," he finally settled on. "Are you all right?"

"I'm fine." She stepped into the room, trying not to show her nervousness when she realized that not only was Evan there, but the rest of the Hansons were, as well.

She tugged the hem of her thin green sweater around her hips and walked to the center of the room. "I'm glad you're all here," she said smoothly. "It saves me from having to make a bunch of phone calls."

"Look, we know we owe you an apology, Helen." Jack spoke first. "Nothing like cooling our heels for a few days to put together some realizations."

"I'm not here for apologies," she assured. "Mori is going to let us know when the meeting will be re-scheduled."

"He still wants to do the deal?" Evan rounded the couch and put his hands over Meredith's shoulders.

"Of course. Why wouldn't he?"

"He didn't exactly give us that impression," David told her. "Guy was pretty pissed."

"Made us feel like a bunch of bratty kids," Andrew added.

"Ones he had no interest in conducting any kind of business with," Evan finished.

Mori had said nothing of the kind to her. But she couldn't let herself think about Mori or she was going to completely lose any semblance of composure. "He would not have spoken of another meeting if that were the case. But before we *do* have the sit-down, I'd like you all to consider something. Before, I'd figured we could deal with the matter after the merger was final— since they are decisions that can be made without TAKA approval. But I realize now there is no time like the present."

"Helen." Samantha came to her side, touching her arm. "You look like you're ready to fall over. Sit down. Please."

"Sam's right. You look like hell. Just what did Taka do to you the last few days?" Andrew pulled a side chair out from the gilt-edged table and carried it over to Helen.

She found herself pushed down into the chair.

What had Mori done to her? He'd made her feel again and she supposed at some point, when she was feeling more…mature about it all, she would feel glad for that and accept all that had happened for what it was.

Right now, she couldn't think about him without her throat closing and her eyes stinging. "I just need a good night of sleep," she said, not even thinking about the impression that statement would make.

"Well, you go, girl," Samantha murmured under her breath, grinning.

All of the women were grinning, in fact. The guys, however, just looked distinctly uncomfortable.

At any other time, Helen might have found the entire matter incredibly amusing.

"That is *not* what I meant," she said evenly, which

unfortunately seemed to have no effect. She pushed at her hair. "What I wanted to discuss was the future. Your future."

Jack picked up the letter from the judge. "I suppose you mean this?"

She nodded. Jack didn't look quite fit to draw and quarter her for her interference. It was something, at least.

"Anyway, when Jack hopefully resumes his practice, I think Evan should assume the head of Hanson North America."

"What?" Evan looked stunned. "Oh hell, yeah. Great idea. That'd have the old man rolling over in his grave."

"George wanted Hanson to continue for *all* of you," Helen said. "I don't know why you can't believe that." She could prove it if she were willing to produce George's letter. Which she wasn't. The humiliation would be more than she could survive.

"That's why he gave you the majority shares," Jack said. "We get it, Helen. He trusted you to do what he figured we wouldn't. Keep Hanson in existence."

"That doesn't mean he'd want me sitting in his old chair," Evan said.

"Does it matter that much to you what George wanted? Think about it, Evan. This is not George's decision. This is yours. All of yours, for that matter."

"I think it's brilliant," Meredith commented.

Evan wasn't so quick to agree, but Helen could see the glint of interest in his eyes. "What about the radio division?" he asked.

"David can take it over." Helen looked toward her brother-in-law. "I know public relations is your thing, David, but I also think it's high time you have your own shop to run. Why not radio? It's either you, or we really will have to sell it off."

"We were prepared for that, anyway," Evan reminded.

"I couldn't keep a seat on the TAKA board and run radio." David looked toward Nina.

"You admitted that you were taking the seat because you felt you needed to, not because you really wanted to," she told him. "Actually, I think it's a marvelous idea, too."

Helen smiled at Nina, grateful for the support. "That just leaves Andrew." She looked up at George's youngest son. "You've proven yourself a powerhouse, Andrew, when it comes to getting new business. If David forfeits his board position, then that leaves you to take it. Are you willing?"

"Maybe *you* should take it," he said, eyeing her speculatively.

She shook her head. "I won't be involved in Hanson after this."

"What do you mean?" Delia sat forward. "You can't just walk away after all of this."

"I'm not walking away," Helen said huskily. "I'll find something to challenge my time. But I'm going to sign my shares equally over to Jack, Evan and Andrew."

"You mean sell them," Evan corrected.

She shook her head. "I meant exactly what I said."

"Don't you want to give some shares to Jenny?"

"I've thought about that, Jack. And the truth is, Jenny doesn't need Hanson shares from me. She needs what she's already realized—that giving her up didn't mean that she was unwanted or unloved by me. Now that I've found her, I have no intention of losing her again. She knows that."

"But what are you going to *do?*" Samantha looked shell-shocked.

Helen looked toward the window. The drapes were open and she could see the clear blue sky outside. "I'll figure something out," she said with much more assurance than she felt. "This is what I want. I just need to know what you all think."

"You don't need our approval," Andrew said.

"She *wants* it," Jack said. "Don't you, Helen." It wasn't a question, but an observation.

And Helen's throat tightened all over again. She hadn't expected anything from the men other than debate and—eventually—seeing the logic of her ways. "Yes."

"I only see one drawback," Evan said.

She should have known it wouldn't be so easy. "What?"

"If you're not involved at Hanson, then you've got nothing to keep you around." He glanced at his brothers. Leaned over and took Meredith's hand in his. "And Meredith and I kind of figured you'd be around for the wedding."

Silence settled on them all for a moment. Then delight struck Helen, giving a seriously hard nudge in reminding her to focus on what was important. "You're getting married! When? Why didn't you say something earlier?"

"We just decided," Meredith said. She looked up at Evan and happiness seemed to radiate from her. "And you *have* to be there, Helen."

"Plus, the baby is going to need a grandma who is way too young for the term," Andrew added, looking wry.

"We were wrong, Helen," Jack said. And his brothers

nodded. "*I* was wrong. No matter what is going on with you and Mori—" he lifted his hand when she opened her mouth to protest "—or not going on, you *are* a Hanson. You are family. *We* are a family, and more. Maybe for the first time. And we owe that to you."

Samantha crouched next to Helen, sliding her arm around her shoulder. "You see? I told you everything would work out."

It seemed that Helen had told Samantha that a time or two. She blinked, but the burning behind her eyes didn't abate. "Okay. Then I guess maybe I won't tell the broker to sell the house, after all. It's a pretty good place to have big old family dinners." Her voice broke a little.

Samantha looked teary, too.

"All right then," David suddenly stood up, clapping his hands together. "Before this gets too damn sappy, I'm starving. What say we get out and try to find some decent sushi?" He grinned.

And everyone laughed.

Even Helen. Which just went to prove, she supposed, that a person could have a broken heart and still find something to smile about.

Helen dressed with extraordinary care for the final meeting with TAKA the next afternoon. If there was one thing she'd learned as Mrs. George Hanson, it was that it was a lot easier to feel impervious when you looked like a million dollars.

The pristine white mandarin-style blouse and severely tailored black jacket and slim skirt fit that particular bill.

"Nervous?"

She was flanked by Jack, Evan, Andrew and David as they walked from the elevator down the corridor to the TAKA boardroom. "No," she lied.

Andrew snorted softly. "Right."

She wasn't nervous about their last bit of business. She *was* nervous about seeing Mori face-to-face. She'd rather kiss a toad than reveal that to anyone, however, most particularly Mori.

When they entered, and Mori was already there, standing near the windows with Shiguro by his side, Helen had to force herself not to turn tail and run.

This was *not* about her feelings for Mori.

This was about the merger.

Period.

She angled her head in a polite bow when his gaze didn't easily release hers and she caught the momentary frown that marred his handsome face before she turned and accepted the filled china teacup offered by a server.

Richard arrived and he joined them for a few minutes before he went over and exchanged pleasantries with the TAKA crew. Because of Jenny, he'd decided to make his stay in Japan permanent and his position had already been outlined during the negotiations. Helen watched him for a moment over the brim of her teacup.

He would do well, she knew. She was completely happy about how things had worked out for him and Jenny, but she knew she would still miss him—as well as Jenny—when she returned to Chicago. He'd been a friend as well as a business associate.

And now, married to Jenny, he was…family.

"You all right?" Evan stepped in front of Helen. "You're looking pale."

"I'm fine." She squeezed his arm and smiled. "It's just been a momentous few days." He'd never know just *how* momentous.

"If we could all be seated," Shiguro announced. "We will begin."

Evan gave her a faint wink and she deposited her half-drunk tea on the tray alongside everyone else's cups and headed toward her usual position next to Jack along the "Hanson" side of the table.

In all of the times since she'd sat at the table, not a single thing had ever been out of place. But Jack's agreement was sitting at her spot. It didn't bear his name, but she clearly recognized his distinctive handwriting on the front of it.

She glanced at his spot, saw her own bound document and casually reached for it, intending to switch the two without drawing undue attention when it was such a minor matter.

Shiguro saw, however. "Mrs. Hanson, you will please to sit where your agreement is located."

She didn't know why she hesitated. She'd spent the past several months working like a fiend to gain that measure of distinction from their opponents.

Shiguro lowered his head slightly. "Please."

Jack moved behind her and nudged her over, pulling the chair out for her. "Go ahead," he encouraged and sat in her typical seat—the "lesser" seat of importance.

Helen slipped into Jack's former seat, keeping her eyes focused within the square of space she was to occupy. If she let her gaze drift even a fraction, she would encounter Mori. She pulled the agreement closer.

This really was it.

The end.

A commotion at the door drew her attention and the jolt of nervousness she suddenly felt barely had time to settle before a video crew—and *not* Yukio with more protests—entered.

She frowned and then did look toward Mori. "What is this?"

"We have much to mark on this occasion," he said. "Footage may be used for the press release announcing the completion of the merger."

She nodded, but she was still surprised. TAKA Corporation might have been a media monster, but when it came to its own internal workings, they were about as tightlipped as it came.

Mori seemed to give the three-person crew no mind, then. "I am certain that you all were expecting another protracted discussion about the guidelines for the Hanson North America's philanthropic interests." He flipped open the book that sat in front of him. "However, you will note that this item has been removed from the stipulations of the merger."

Helen's attention sharpened. Adrenaline surged through her veins. "You can't tell me that you're retracting the sixty percent you were previously willing to agree to?"

Mori's dark gaze locked with hers, but it was Shiguro who answered. "TAKA has determined that such a decision will remain within the local management of Hanson North America," he said.

Silence screamed from Hanson's side of the table.

A complete capitulation was so extraordinarily out of character that Helen didn't know *what* to say. She stared at Mori. Finally, one word emerged. "Why?"

"You may accept the decision as a sign of confidence in the new management."

"Sounds good to me," Andrew said wryly from farther down the table.

Cautious chuckles from the other side of the table followed.

"Speaking of management," Helen said, "there may be some shifting around. The only portion of that which needs to be addressed here, though, is the possibility of Andrew Hanson taking the TAKA board position in place of David Hanson."

"It's more than a possibility," Evan told her, leaning forward to look at her from his position next to Andrew. "We all talked last night, Helen. I'll be assuming Jack's position and David will resign from Hanson North America to assume control of the newly independent broadcasting company. Which means Andrew has to take the board position."

"I didn't expect such a quick decision from you all," Helen admitted faintly.

"You're not the only one who can move decisively," Andrew drawled, but he was smiling as he said it.

Helen folded her hands tightly together in her lap beneath cover of the table. She nodded, too full of emotion to speak just then.

"Andrew Hanson will assume the third board position, then," Mori said.

"Unless Helen wants it," Andrew interrupted.

"Helen cannot hold a position on the TAKA board of directors," Mori said smoothly.

Even though Helen knew a woman—particularly *her*—would never be allowed on the TAKA board, hearing it drop so easily from his lips still pained her.

"Not yet," Mori added.

She jerked and stared at him. Not *yet?* "What is that supposed to mean?"

"Patience." He looked down the table. "TAKA has added a condition of our own to the document. You will find the addendum inserted before the final page." He barely waited while pages rustled as people hurried to catch up with the unexpected.

Helen was no different. She flipped to the back of the hefty document and found the page. She was vaguely aware of the video crew moving discreetly closer to the table and its occupants.

"TAKA wishes to name Helen Hanson as Senior Vice President of TAKA mergers and acquisitions," Mori announced. "This means she will no longer be part of Hanson management, but part of TAKA." He was no longer looking at anyone else.

He was only looking at Helen.

"If she chooses to accept, of course," he finished.

The only sound in the room was the faint tick of someone's watch.

Helen swallowed. There was not a single female who held a senior management position within TAKA. "You're serious," she finally managed.

"It is in black and white for all the world to witness." He reached into his lapel pocket and pulled out a familiar pen.

Her gold pen.

He extended it to her. "Perhaps you have need for this, Mrs. Hanson." He smiled slightly.

Biting her lip, she looked at Jack. Then Richard, Evan, David. Andrew. All of these people who'd come to mean more to her in the past several months than she could have wished for.

Andrew's arms were crossed over his wide chest when she looked at him and his hand shifted slightly. His thumb popped up.

Could she work for TAKA? Could she function day in and day out within the confines of their strictly defined behaviors and ideologies?

Then she looked at Mori again.

What he was doing was already counterpoint to all of that, she realized. And if that wasn't proof that TAKA's internal practices were no longer set in stone, she couldn't fathom what would be.

"Some things are meant to be," he said quietly, still holding out the pen.

Even though they had a room full of witnesses, Helen couldn't simply leave it at that. Not when her *life* was finding paths she had never considered. "Which things? A career with TAKA? Or being with you? You didn't say a word about this when I suggested I might like to stay on in Tokyo."

"I asked why you wanted to do so," he reminded her. "You chose not to answer."

"I couldn't understand how you could ask the question in the first place, after we'd—" She broke off, flushing, suddenly painfully aware that not only were there witnesses, but there was a video crew taping the entire exchange. "Would it have mattered to you what reason I had?"

"Yes. But it would not change the offer on the table today. You are a worthy opponent, Mrs. Hanson. I prefer to make allies of such people and turn their abilities to my benefit. You will be breaking new ground for TAKA," Mori said. "I cannot assure you that it will always be easy. You are too intelligent a woman to believe otherwise. The question is, are you willing?"

She slowly took the pen from Mori and their fingers grazed. *"Hai."*

While the video camera moved closer, Helen turned to the last and final page of the merger agreement.

Mori had already signed it.

She stared at his signature, her hand tightly holding on to George's pen.

Maybe George's behavior hadn't been as selfishly calculated as she'd believed. Maybe, just maybe, he'd somehow been watching out for her, all along.

It was a good thought. A very good thought. One that she figured she'd just have to hold on to.

She let out a little breath.

And she signed her name.

Mori nodded, clearly satisfied. He took the document from her, closed it with great care and stood to look around the table. "Now, finally, we will adjourn to the lobby and celebrate. Mrs. Hanson and I will join you shortly."

Even the TAKA side looked relieved, clapping their hands together as spontaneously as the Hanson side as men pushed back from the table and rose, shaking hands and bowing and generally congratulating each other. Laughter and voices grew more enthusiastic and less restrained as people—no longer teams on opposing sides, but people who'd ultimately succeeded in a common effort—began filing out of the boardroom.

Helen rose, also, though she wasn't entirely certain her wobbling legs would serve the task. "Well." She moistened her lips. "I guess you are my boss now. I'll have to learn how not to debate every point with you."

"I do not wish you to change your methods, Helen. They are already admirable. You will need to learn to speak Japanese more fluently, of course, but you will have much assistance for that. The only other thing I wish you to change is your name."

She blinked. "My name? Whatever for? You don't want a *Hanson* on the TAKA staff roster?"

"Do you not understand yet?" He looked vaguely amused as he took the pen from her that she hadn't realized she still held and set it on the table.

Her frayed nerves were in danger of complete disintegration. She looked around, but everyone had deserted them.

"It is just you and me," he said, clearly reading her mind. He took her hands in his and whatever amusement he'd shown was now utterly absent. "I wish for you not to be Hanson-san, but Taka-san."

She swayed and his grip tightened, steadying. "I'm sorry. I don't think I heard you right."

"I think you did," he countered gently. "I want you to be my wife."

His words hovered between them like some tantalizing wish. "But you just gave me a job!"

"We cannot work together yet be married?"

"George certainly never thought so," she said faintly.

"I am not George Hanson."

No. He wasn't. He'd been proving it again and again and again.

How much more would she need to believe in that?

"I once thought you were just like him," she admitted. "I was wrong. But, Mori, you're not going to win points with some people. I don't know which will strike them as more inflammatory. Employing me, or marrying me."

"Who is *them?*"

She shook her head, feeling oddly panicked. "I don't know. Your father, for one."

"He is a traditional man but the world we inhabit is not so traditional any longer. In time, he will adjust."

"But…marriage? Why marriage? Couldn't we just… be together?"

His dimple appeared. "I do not wish a mistress, Helen. I want a wife. A puzzling, intriguing, challenging American wife named Helen Hanson. I want Kimiko to have a mother named Helen Hanson. She agrees."

Her vision blurred with sudden tears. "You've talked to Kimiko about us?"

"Yes."

"What did you tell her?"

He stepped closer. "I told her that I loved you."

She pressed her lips together to stop them from trembling. "You *do?*"

"Yes. I love you. Why else would I ask you to be my wife?"

"People marry for all sorts of reasons."

"You do not. You only marry for love, remember?"

"I remember." She dragged in a shaking breath. "Are

you *sure?* I couldn't survive it if you changed your mind along the way."

"Do you love me, Helen?"

The tears finally spilled from the corners of her eyes. "Yes. I love you. I never expected it, but I do."

"Will you be changing your mind along the way?"

She shook her head knowing down in her soul that what she felt for this man would never cease. "No."

"Then trust me as I will trust you. I will not change my mind." He skimmed his hand down her cheek, wiping away her tears. "Do I need to put *that* in writing for you, as well?"

She slipped her arms around his neck. "Maybe," she whispered.

He reared his head back. His eyebrows drew together, making him look dark and fierce. "What?"

She smiled softly. "I assume even in Japan there is a marriage license that will need to be signed."

His eyes narrowed. Then his expression eased. A smile slowly curved his mouth. "You are agreeing? Kimiko lectured me for an hour that I must do this most perfectly. That I had to take you somewhere romantic. Give you flowers and sweets and bend on my knees like they do in the movies."

"Kimiko is twelve," Helen said huskily. "We met here in this boardroom so I think your choice was quite perfect. And yes. I am agreeing." She pressed her lips softly to his, grasping with both hands for their future. "I love you, Morito Taka. And I wish for you to be my husband."

"I was not sure what you would say."

Her heart ached at his gruff admission. "I don't argue

the really good ideas," she whispered. "And I'll give it a little while before I tell you that I think Kimiko should be living with her father and not at school."

"Do you think my daughter has not already realized that?" He caught her face in his hands and kissed her thoroughly.

She slid her arms beneath his jacket, fitting herself even more closely against him.

He inhaled sharply. "I am grateful the video crew has gone and that there is not a security camera in this room."

Helen couldn't help herself. She looked at the wide, sturdy surface of the conference table. "Really."

"*That* would be a merger the likes of which the table has never seen."

She slid her hands slowly up his spine and back down again and looked up at him from beneath her lashes. *"Never?"*

"Well." His dark eyes glinted. "Not yet, Mrs. Hanson. Not…just…yet."

Epilogue

"She looks beautiful, doesn't she? I wasn't sure we would live to see the day."

"Aw, come on. They're meant to be."

"I hear they're living in Japan."

"Hope they like sushi."

Helen listened to the whispered conversations behind her and hid a smile.

"Oh, my God. Is Meredith *barefoot?*"

"I'm still surprised she and Evan didn't get married right out of high school."

Mori leaned his head close to Helen's as they watched Evan take Meredith's hand when she joined him in front of the minister. The music, courtesy of a trio of steel drums, had not yet ceased. "Do all American weddings necessitate incessant whispering from the guests?" he asked.

She slipped her hand into his. "I'm afraid Hanson weddings probably do," she whispered back.

"Did they whisper like this at *our* wedding?"

"Probably. You didn't notice?"

"I was busy watching my bride," he murmured.

"Well, if it's any help, I didn't notice, either. I was too busy watching my groom. He was very handsome in his kimono." She lowered her voice even more. "I was curious what all he wore beneath it. Turned out...not much." The steel drums finally faded into silence.

The sun was just beginning to set and color filled the Caribbean sky, almost matching the vivid colors of the orchids that wreathed Meredith's and her attendants' heads. It was she, proving she had more "free spirit" inside her than people thought, who had chosen the little island destination for her and Evan's wedding. Despite the location, however, there were close to a hundred people who'd flown in for the event.

Mori slipped his arm around Helen's shoulders and she sighed, leaning against him contentedly as she watched the couple exchange vows and thought about *their* wedding in Nesutotaka two months earlier.

It had been a mix of traditional and Western, just as their life together was. She and Mori had worn traditional Japanese wedding garb. Jack, Evan and Andrew—all in black suits—had given her away. Kimiko, Helen's flower girl, had worn a long pink dress with spaghetti straps that her father had groaned over. When the official teenager hadn't been preening in her dress to Zach, Nina's twelve-year-old son, she'd been chasing around with Izzy, Nina's ten-year-old youngest. Samantha, Meredith and Nina had worn summery dresses of their own choosing, and Jenny had worn a pale green suit that had masked her new pregnancy.

Nesutotaka had bulged at the seams with the guests who'd traveled there for the ceremony, and of course, every person who lived in the village had been present. Even Yukio Taka, who'd finally stopped openly disapproving of Helen and had taken to sending her e-mails regarding troubled companies he figured TAKA needed to be looking at. Ideas which he seemed to delight in fiercely debating with her.

"Would you rather have had a wedding like this?" Mori asked as they watched Evan slide a narrow band on Meredith's finger.

"I loved our wedding," Helen assured. "But it wasn't the wedding that really mattered. It's the life spent together that does."

"Do you think they know that?" He nodded toward the new couple as they sealed their exchanges with a kiss that went on long enough to have Evan's brothers and uncle who stood on his side of the sand, and their wives who stood on Meredith's side, grinning wryly.

Kimiko, not officially part of the wedding party, but still wearing a matching wreath of orchids in her hair, tugged on Helen's wrist. "When do we get to go scuba diving?" she whispered when Helen looked at her.

"Tomorrow." Helen promised, whispering back. On the other side of Kimi, Jenny stood holding hands with Richard. She'd caught Kimi's question and was smiling.

A balmy breeze drifted over them and Helen closed her hand over Kimi's and leaned her head against her husband's shoulder. She looked at Evan and Meredith as they joined hands and smiled broadly as they walked away from the minister, their bare feet sinking into the soft white sand. Behind them, the rest of the Hanson men found their mates and followed.

"Yes," Helen answered. "I think they *all* know that is what's really important. They are living proof of it."

Mori angled his head and brushed his lips over hers. "You are crying."

She smiled at him, not even trying to hide the moisture that had filled her eyes. "Happy tears, Mori. I promise. Always happy tears."

* * * * *

HOTEL MARCHAND

**Four sisters.
A family legacy.
And someone is out to destroy it.**

**A captivating new limited
continuity, launching June 2006**

The most beautiful hotel in New Orleans,
and someone is out to destroy it. But mystery,
danger and some surprising family revelations
and discoveries won't stop the Marchand sisters
from protecting their birthright…
and finding love along the way.

HOTEL MARCHAND

SPECIAL PRICE!

This riveting new saga begins with

In the Dark

by national bestselling author

JUDITH ARNOLD

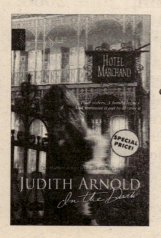

The party at Hotel Marchand is in full swing when the lights suddenly go out. What does head of security Mac Jensen do first? He's torn between two jobs—protecting the guests at the hotel and keeping the woman he loves safe.

A woman to protect. A hotel to secure. And no idea who's determined to harm them.

On Sale June 2006

HMITD

Page-turning drama...

Exotic, glamorous locations...

Intense emotion and passionate seduction...

Sheikhs, princes and billionaire tycoons...

This summer, may we suggest:

**THE SHEIKH'S
DISOBEDIENT BRIDE**
by Jane Porter
On sale June.

**AT THE GREEK TYCOON'S
BIDDING**
by Cathy Williams
On sale July.

**THE ITALIAN MILLIONAIRE'S
VIRGIN WIFE**
On sale August.

With new titles to choose from every month,
discover a world of romance in our books written
by internationally bestselling authors.

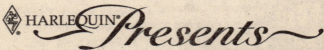

It's the ultimate in quality romance!

Available wherever Harlequin books are sold.

www.eHarlequin.com

HPGEN06

If you enjoyed what you just read,
then we've got an offer you can't resist!

Take 2 bestselling love stories FREE!
Plus get a FREE surprise gift!

Clip this page and mail it to Silhouette Reader Service™

IN U.S.A.	IN CANADA
3010 Walden Ave.	P.O. Box 609
P.O. Box 1867	Fort Erie, Ontario
Buffalo, N.Y. 14240-1867	L2A 5X3

YES! Please send me 2 free Silhouette Special Edition® novels and my free surprise gift. After receiving them, if I don't wish to receive anymore, I can return the shipping statement marked cancel. If I don't cancel, I will receive 6 brand-new novels every month, before they're available in stores! In the U.S.A., bill me at the bargain price of $4.24 plus 25¢ shipping and handling per book and applicable sales tax, if any*. In Canada, bill me at the bargain price of $4.99 plus 25¢ shipping and handling per book and applicable taxes**. That's the complete price and a savings of at least 10% off the cover prices—what a great deal! I understand that accepting the 2 free books and gift places me under no obligation ever to buy any books. I can always return a shipment and cancel at any time. Even if I never buy another book from Silhouette, the 2 free books and gift are mine to keep forever.

235 SDN DZ9D
335 SDN DZ9E

Name	(PLEASE PRINT)
Address	Apt.#
City	State/Prov. Zip/Postal Code

Not valid to current Silhouette Special Edition® subscribers.

Want to try two free books from another series?
Call 1-800-873-8635 or visit www.morefreebooks.com.

* Terms and prices subject to change without notice. Sales tax applicable in N.Y.
** Canadian residents will be charged applicable provincial taxes and GST.
All orders subject to approval. Offer limited to one per household.
® are registered trademarks owned and used by the trademark owner or its licensee.

SPED04R   ©2004 Harlequin Enterprises Limited

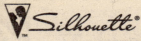
SPECIAL EDITION

#1765 THE RELUCTANT CINDERELLA—Christine Rimmer
Talk of the Town
When humble business owner Megan Schumacher landed the
Banning's department store account, she landed Greg Banning, too.
He loved her ideas for updating the company's image—and couldn't get
the image of this sexy woman out of his head. But the town gossips had
a field day—and Greg's ex-wife, who'd introduced the pair,
wasn't amused....

#1766 PRINCESS IN DISGUISE—Lilian Darcy
Wanted: Outback Wives
Tired of her philandering fiancé, jet-setting Princess Misha decided
to unwind at a remote sheep farm in Australia. But when she arrived,
farmer Brant Smith mistook her for one of the candidates a local
woman's magazine had been sending him as a possible wife! Perhaps
the down-to-earth royal fit the bill more than either of them first
suspected....

#1767 THE BABY TRAIL—Karen Rose Smith
Baby Bonds
Finding a stranger's baby in her sunroom, Gwen Longworthy resolved
to reunite mother and child, since she knew all too well the pain of
separation. Luckily she had former FBI agent Garrett Maxwell to help
search for the mother...and soothe Gwen's own wounded heart.

#1768 THE TENANT WHO CAME TO STAY—Pamela Toth
Reunited
Taking in male boarder Wade Garrett was a stretch for
Pauline Mayfield—falling in love with him really turned heads!
And just when Pauline had all the drama she could take, her estranged
sister, Lily, showed up, with child in tow and nowhere to go. The
more the merrier...or would Lily get up to her old tricks and make
a play for Pauline's man?

#1769 AT THE MILLIONAIRE'S REQUEST—Teresa Southwick
When millionaire Gavin Spencer needed a speech therapist for his
injured son, he asked for M. J. Taylor's help. But the job reminded M.J.
of the tragic loss of her own child, and her proximity to Gavin raised
trust issues for them both. As the boy began to heal, would M.J. and
Gavin follow suit—and give voice to their growing feelings for each
other?

#1770 SECOND-TIME LUCKY—Laurie Paige
Canyon Country
How ironic that family counselor Caileen Peters had so much
trouble keeping her own daughter in line. And that Caileen was
turning to her client Jefferson Aquilon, a veteran raising two orphans,
for help. But mother and daughter both found inspiration in the Aquilon
household—and Caileen soon found something more in Jefferson's
arms.

SSECNM0606